For my favourite son

PUFFIN BOOKS

SPY DOG
CAPTURED!

Andrew Cope lives with his wife and two children in a small town near Derby. He really does have a dog called Lara, who has one sticky-up ear and came from the RSPCA. He suspects she could be a secret agent but she hides her identity well.

Andrew runs a training course called 'The Art of Being Brilliant' for businesses and schools. If you would like him to come and talk to pupils, teachers and parents at your school, please email him at andy@artofbrilliance.co.uk. He may even be able to bring Lara!

SPY DOG
CAPTURED!

ANDREW COPE

Illustrated by Chris Mould

PUFFIN

PUFFIN BOOKS

Published by the Penguin Group
Penguin Books Ltd, 80 Strand, London WC2R 0RL, England
Penguin Group (USA) Inc., 375 Hudson Street, New York, New York 10014, USA
Penguin Group (Canada), 90 Eglinton Avenue East, Suite 700, Toronto, Ontario, Canada M4P 2Y3
(a division of Pearson Penguin Canada Inc.)
Penguin Ireland, 25 St Stephen's Green, Dublin 2, Ireland (a division of Penguin Books Ltd)
Penguin Group (Australia), 250 Camberwell Road, Camberwell, Victoria 3124, Australia
(a division of Pearson Australia Group Pty Ltd)
Penguin Books India Pvt Ltd, 11 Community Centre, Panchsheel Park, New Delhi – 110 017, India
Penguin Group (NZ), 67 Apollo Drive, Rosedale, Auckland 0632, New Zealand
(a division of Pearson New Zealand Ltd)
Penguin Books (South Africa) (Pty) Ltd, 24 Sturdee Avenue, Rosebank, Johannesburg 2196, South Africa

Penguin Books Ltd, Registered Offices: 80 Strand, London WC2R 0RL, England

www.penguin.com

First published 2006
017

Text copyright © Andrew Cope, 2006
Illustrations copyright © Chris Mould, 2006
All rights reserved

The moral right of the author and illustrator has been asserted

Set in Bembo
Typeset by Palimpsest Book Production Limited, Falkirk, Stirlingshire
Made and printed in Great Britain by Clays Ltd, St Ives plc

British Library Cataloguing in Publication Data
A CIP catalogue record for this book is available from the British Library

ISBN-13: 978–0–141–31885–1
ISBN-10: 0–141–31885–6

www.greenpenguin.co.uk

Thanks to:

Lou
For understanding and patience.

Mum
For the crucial idea. If it was so obvious,
why didn't I think of it?

The Thursday-night boys
For not taking me too seriously.

Elv and the Puffin team
For help, support and some great ideas..

Goldfields Academy, South Africa
For the inspirational days and quiet evenings.

Contents

1. Hounding the Opposition

The villagers had crammed into the sports hall for the match. It was strictly an invited audience of local residents and leisure-centre staff. Dad had acted as doorman, checking identification to make sure there were no prying eyes.

With two minutes to go, the game was on a knife-edge as the boys' top scorer stepped up to take a penalty. He tried to stay cool as he placed the ball on the spot, knowing that if he could stick this penalty away it would win the match for them and save his reputation.

All the players retreated to the edge of the area and waited for the referee to blow his whistle. The spectators were open-mouthed and silent. The top scorer looked at his team-mates' faces, glowing with sweat and effort. If they lost to the girls they would be glowing red with embarrassment. He glanced at the referee. The whistle echoed around the sports hall. It was now him against the girls' goalkeeper. She was gorilla-like on the goal line, waving her arms up and down, trying to put him off.

He ran forward four paces and made excellent contact. The ball flew towards the top left-hand corner. Perfect. But the goalie had dived the right way, tipping the ball on to the post. It rebounded to safety and another of the girls hoofed it upfield. The game was still alive and children hared down the sports hall in search of the decider. One of the yellow-bibbed girls got the ball on the wing and shaped to cross. The girls' goalkeeper, fresh from the glory of her penalty save, was sprinting up the pitch. She raised her arm. *Me, me, me,* she urged. *Cross it to me and I'll score the winner.* The cross floated into the crowded area and heads rose to connect with the ball. The boys' top scorer reached the highest, trying to make up for his penalty miss. The ball bounced off the back of his head and looped into the air. The girls' keeper had timed her run

to perfection. From the moment she caught the ball on the volley there was no doubt where it was going. The boys' goalie was rooted to the spot as the ball billowed into the corner of his net.

And it's there! howled the scorer. *Another terrific strike from the girl wonder.*

She slid across the floor on her belly, like she'd seen Premiership footballers do, before disappearing under a pile of players. The boys were a picture of defeat. How could they lose to a bunch of girls?

The girls eventually recovered their composure.

'Our game I believe, gentlemen,' said Sophie, the team captain. 'Perhaps we can arrange a rematch? Or are you afraid we might humiliate you even more next time?'

The opposing captain couldn't think of a reply. The embarrassment was too much. The teams exchanged handshakes or, in the case of the girls' goalkeeper, paws. The goalie and winning scorer was in fact Lara, Sophie's pet dog.

'Excellent game, Lara,' said Sophie. 'Your

goalkeeping kept us in the match and that winner was a bit special.'

Lara wagged furiously as she slipped off her goalie gloves. *Thanks*, she thought. *I did catch it rather well. My game is certainly improving. Bring on Man U!*

The newspaper photographer crept back into the broom cupboard. He removed his fake identity badge, smiling to himself as he threw it into the bin. He quickly packed his camera away, delighted that he'd snapped the mutt in mid-volley. The story would be worth thousands and the pictures even more. He smiled at his genius. Going undercover as a leisure-centre member of staff had worked a treat. He changed out of the staff uniform he'd 'borrowed' and peeped out of the cupboard. The coast was clear, so he casually strode past reception and out of the building. He even had the confidence to nod to the lady on reception.

He got into a red car and grinned at his mate. 'A result.' He beamed. 'If gathering evidence is going to be this easy, we'll have our story within days.'

2. The Domestic Goddess

The newspaper reporters were being very careful. They needed to get more shots of the footballing mutt, but didn't want to get caught. One sat in a tree and focused his long telephoto lens on the house, while the other was struggling into his postman's outfit. The dog came into view, apparently making a cup of tea. Tree-man zoomed in . . . click, click, click.

Lara put two heaped teaspoons of cocoa powder into a mug and stirred. She cradled the mug in her paws and walked into the lounge, placing her drink on the table while it cooled. She picked a pen up in her mouth and finished the crossword. *Sixteen across . . . fictional secret agent . . . five and four . . . a doddle,* she thought, filling in the spaces

with 'James' and 'Bond'. *He was a spy too.*

She recalled being allocated her real name, GM451, a title given to her by the British Secret Service. It was the Secret Service that had reared her and invested in advanced learning techniques. Lara actually stood for 'Licensed Assault and Rescue Animal' and she was the canine equivalent of James Bond. Except, of course, that 007 is terribly good-looking and sophisticated, two characteristics that Lara lacked. *It's not that I'm ugly, more unusual*, she thought. She was about the size of a Labrador, mostly white with large black patches splashed over her body and face. In fact, her markings were a bit like a cow's, although she was offended when her owners pointed this out. *A cow indeed! They are dirty, smelly, stupid creatures with muck all over their tails. Me, on the other hand, well, I have a shower every morning and I'm super-intelligent and toilet-trained.*

Lara caught her reflection in the mirror. *Mmm . . . definitely unusual.* She had spiky black and white whiskers but her most distinctive feature was her ears. One flopped over her eye and the other stood upright. She put her paw to the sticky-up ear and felt the bullet hole. She shuddered as she recalled the encounter with the gunman just a few months ago. She also walked with a slight limp, another souvenir of her recent adventure. Lara had a bullet embedded in her thigh, wedged in so deep the vet had decided it was safer to leave it than operate.

Lara flicked on the TV but couldn't settle. She had a nagging feeling that she was being watched. She wandered over to the window, put her paws on the sill and stared out into the garden. The photographer stopped clicking and nearly fell out of his tree in alarm. He sat perfectly still, hoping his green jacket would keep him hidden.

Lara scanned the garden and the parked cars in the road. The red Ford went unnoticed. *Nothing. Must be imagining things.* She wandered back to the sofa just in time to catch the news headlines. *The same old troubles in the world*, she thought. There was a piece about education and she smiled to herself as she reflected on her first year at spy school. *I mastered English, French and German as well as a bit of Chinese. After just a few months I could understand more vocabulary than the average human, which is pretty impressive for a dog.* She ran through a bit of French in her head. Oui, *it's still there.* She smiled. Lara's biggest frustration was that she could only speak one language – her native tongue of Dog. She would have loved to learn to speak Human but this was beyond the spy-training programme. *But I can work a laptop and send emails using a pencil in my mouth to tap out the letters. I'm a keen sports dog. I am excellent at football, gymnastics, swimming and karate. I can drive, navigate, ride* a horse and defuse a bomb. *I am also intelligent enough to do jigsaws, play chess and write poetry. I mean, how many dogs can do that?* she considered. *I've got straight As in maths, English and science. In fact, the only exam I've ever failed is music, because it's difficult to play the piano properly with these.* She held up her paws. *I guess they do make me a bit clumsy,* she sighed, wiggling her claws, wishing they were more like fingers. She flicked the remote and settled on a quiz show. *Too easy.* She could always answer the questions on *Millionaire* and, should he ever get picked, was on Professor Cortex's 'phone a friend' list. *He says I can bark the answer to A, B, C or D,* she thought proudly.

Lara trotted back to the kitchen and fetched the biscuit tin. She recalled the day that she'd been released from the Secret Service. *One of the best days of my life, without a doubt.* She smiled. *Being a secret agent was good, but being a pet is brilliant.* She put the unopened biscuit tin on the table and eyed it longingly. *I shouldn't really,* she thought, remembering her diet.

★

The doorbell rang. *Mmm . . . what should I do?* she thought. *I'm supposed to be a normal dog and most dogs don't answer the door.* She peeped through the net curtain and saw it was the postman. *Not the usual one,* she observed. *But I expect he's local so he knows my secret.* She trotted to the front door, jumped up and pulled the handle.

'Err, Special Delivery,' said the postman, apparently relaxed at seeing a dog answer the door. 'Can you sign here?' Lara took his pen in her mouth and signed the paperwork. 'Thanks very much, err, La-la,' he mumbled, squinting at her signature.

No problem, Mr Postie. Lara nodded at him and took the parcel, closing the door behind her. She went back into the lounge and ripped open the box. It was a clock, with a card from Auntie Elsie. *How very kind*, thought Lara, making room on the mantelpiece, before sipping the last of her cocoa.

Lara chose a DVD and waited while it loaded.

She remembered the deal she'd struck with the Secret Service. She could return to the Cooks as a family pet as long as she tried her best to behave normally, like any other dog. *But what is 'normal', anyway? Surely I'm allowed to show off a little?*

The DVD came on and she settled comfortably into the armchair. It was a cops and robbers film and her heart raced as she thought about all the crimes she had managed to solve. She recalled her first family mission . . . *to blend into the background, acting like an ordinary domestic pet rather than a highly trained secret agent. But my cover was blown and the whole family were lured into danger, hence the bullet wounds. So this time I'm going to be more careful. Mind you, all the local residents already know I'm a bit special, so why hide myself away? They've seen me on the news, as well as driving a car in the village. If I feel like the occasional game of five-a-side football, then so be it. After all, it was behind closed doors. If I feel like going to judo lessons at the leisure centre, I will. If I want to go to the gym, what the heck! I suppose some people might say I'm showing off, but to me it's normal. I've made a promise not to flaunt my skills outside the village. No picking fights with other dogs, no drawing unnecessary attention to the neighbourhood and absolutely no getting into the newspapers. In fact, the village community love having me around and are happy to keep my special skills secret.*

Lara was proud of her achievements since moving into the neighbourhood. *Let's look at the facts,* she thought. *I've more or less stamped out crime around here. Teenagers know better than to misbehave in the village centre. There's absolutely no litter dropped, and even burglars have got the message. The village is the safest, cleanest and happiest it has ever been – all thanks to yours truly, the one and only canine special agent.* Her bullet-holed ear stood prouder than ever. There had been a bit of a local news splash early on, but it had all died down and the residents knew better than to create more publicity. *My secret's safe with them.*

The undercover reporter entered the office and removed his postman's outfit, satisfied with having successfully completed phase two of his plan. 'Even easier than I thought.' He grinned at his colleague. 'And look at this, I even got the mutt's autograph.'

He switched on the TV and fiddled with

the remote until a picture of Lara's living room was beamed on to his screen. Auntie Elsie's clock contained a secret camera that was now safely in the dog's house. The pair were delighted that the picture was so sharp. Now they could spy on the family twenty-four hours a day. 'Perfect delivery,' chuckled the pretend postman. 'It's absolutely first class.'

The reporters watched open-mouthed as Lara lay face down and did fifty press-ups. Next she stood and did a dozen star jumps. *That's better*, she thought, as she opened the biscuit tin and helped herself to a couple of custard creams. *I think I've earned them now.*

She glanced at the picture of the children on the mantelpiece and felt a warm glow on the inside. *And look how well I've adapted to family life. OK, I had a sticky start and, admittedly it's not as exciting as being a spy, but there comes a time to hang up your gadgets and settle down. There are no airs and graces and I'm treated like one of the family rather than a special agent, but there's love, gallons of the stuff, and that makes me grin, it really does. Life is fantastic.*

Lara the domestic dog goddess stretched out on the sofa for her nap. *I've watched a DVD, finished the crossword and read a couple of chapters of my book. It doesn't get any better than this.*

Little did Lara know that her cosy life was about to be transformed into one of excitement and adventure.

3. Lying in Wait

The man with the telephoto lens shuffled his bottom, trying to get more comfortable. He glanced at his watch and sighed. He had been in hiding since dawn and needed some action pretty soon if he and his colleague were to make their fortunes. The bush hid him well, with just the long camera lens poking out. He shifted again, removing a twig from his ear. A bird landed in the bush, pooped on his shoulder and took off again. The man cursed. He was uncomfortable and hungry, but he wasn't about to give up.

His friend came into view, walking up the path towards the house carrying three pints of milk. 'Yesterday Postman Pat and today Mr Milko,' grinned the camera man. 'I do hope they like today's delivery.' He watched

as his colleague lingered on the doorstep, pretending to deliver the milk, knowing that he was really leaving a small microphone. The pretend milkman then walked away from the house, whistling loudly. He winked at the bush as he went by, his job done.

'Perfect,' whispered the photographer. 'This is all so easy.' It had taken them months of painstaking work to get this far. He remembered seeing the dog carrying out a daring rescue that had made the *News at Ten*. He'd teamed up with the best undercover reporter he could find and followed up the story, but the trail had gone cold, as if someone was trying to hide the truth. Why would nobody tell them about this dog? 'Super Dog' they'd called her on the news. 'Mystery Dog' more like. They smelt a story and the more people avoided them the more their curiosity grew. Their investigations had drawn them towards this village and here the mystery deepened. It wasn't a normal village. There was no litter and no crime. And where was the graffiti? Nobody locked their houses at night. Car doors were left open yet nobody ever had their vehicle stolen. Everyone trusted their neighbours. It just wasn't right. They had discovered there hadn't been a single reported crime in the last six months and the local police station had closed.

The reporters had asked about the dog in the village and everyone had been cagey, as if they were hiding a big secret. Like all newspaper reporters they hated secrets. They had an appetite for an exclusive story and phase one at the leisure centre had just been the starter. Phase two meant their spy camera was now safely in the house. Phase three was this stake-out. They knew they would have to be patient. They believed that good things always came to those who waited.

The photographer stiffened as the Cooks' front door opened and out came Ben, Sophie and the dog. This could be his chance. The camera whirred into action. Perfect one of the boy, then the girl, now the dog. Click, click, click.

They walked right past his hiding place and he stopped clicking, sitting silently while they went by. Because he knew she was a special dog, he had taken care to smear himself with dirt, commando-style, so the blasted mutt wouldn't sniff him out. It was a bit smelly but he didn't care. He knew that if he could get photographic evidence of the dog's special abilities they would be able to sell his snaps to the highest bidder and he would be made forever. The pictures would be worth thousands to the Sunday tabloids. He smiled at the thought.

He held his breath as they went by. Ben held his too. 'Pooheee, Lara, what's that smell? Stinks like dog dirt. You've not been pooing in the garden, have you?'

Certainly not, Lara thought, shaking her head furiously. *What a disgusting thought. I always take care to go to the bathroom. It must be someone else's dog.* Lara approached the bush to investigate the strong smell and the photographer nearly had a panic attack. How would he explain to the neighbours why he had been sitting in a bush, smeared in mud, taking snapshots of the local children? Instead of taking pictures for the news, he would be in the news. This could be the

first crime to hit the village in a year. And what if the dog turned nasty? After all, his investigation had revealed her to be a judo black belt. The dog was just about to poke her nose into the bush when Ben called out, 'Come on, Lara, let's go and see if Brad and Connor have turned up for tennis. They said ten o'clock, so we'll have to hurry.'

Ben fastened the helmet strap under his chin and jumped on his bike. He sped away, pedalling furiously to catch up with his sister. To the photographer's amazement, Lara also jumped on a bike and pedalled after the children, ears flapping in the wind. The camera whirred into action. Click, click, click. *A cycling dog. Now that's a secret that's worth sharing with the world,* he thought.

4. Inspecting Gadgets

'Well, he'd better not be trying to take Lara away,' shouted Ben when he heard the news.

Dad tried to calm him. 'Don't worry, mate. He said he just needed to drop by to offer Lara some extra security. Remember when she was tracked by that horrible man, the drug criminal, who nearly killed her? There are some governments who would give lots of money to get their hands on a spy dog – even if she is a bit damaged.'

A bit damaged! thought Lara indignantly. *He's making me sound like something that's dropped off the back of a lorry!*

'If the professor can make Lara a bit safer, then so be it.'

'Well, she's not going anywhere,' reminded Ben as he stormed out, slamming the door behind him. Lara put her headphones back on and turned her iPod up. *I agree with Ben,* she thought. *There's no way I'm leaving family life.*

Lara suspected that Ben loved her the most. Of all the family, he was the one who had bonded with her best and they had become bosom pals. Lara knew she was the family pet and tried to share her affection around, but she had a fierce loyalty to Ben. *I love his positive attitude to life and his sense of humour,* she thought. He was a handsome boy with fair hair that was always kept long to hide his big ears. Lara knew Ben was popular at school. He was definitely 'one of the lads'. Lara thought it amusing that he didn't realize quite how popular he was with the girls too. His name appeared on several of the girls' pencil cases as well as on their changing-room wall. Most of all, she appreciated the fact that Ben was the one who made a special effort to play outside with her. *I really love it when we get to go outside for a kick-about, even on rainy days. My crosses are getting better and his headers have improved no end.* Lara's real strength was her goalkeeping. *I absolutely love putting the goalie gloves on and standing between the posts while Ben fires shots at me.* She puffed out her chest as she remembered leaping across the goalmouth, tipping the ball away one-pawed. *And then we come indoors, steaming and muddy, and sit in front of a DVD. Ours is most definitely a special relationship.*

Lara had also bonded with Ben's younger sister and brother. Sophie was a couple of years younger, her cheeky face and sparkly eyes giving away her delight at having her own pet dog. Lara tried to be the perfect homework companion. *I do earn my keep,* she thought. *I mean, how many pets help with difficult maths problems and listen patiently while their owners read their library book. And the hours I spend with Sophie, drawing and colouring with her.* Lara had to hold the pencil in her mouth, a technique that Sophie would sometimes try to copy. While Lara expertly gripped the pencil in her mouth, Sophie slobbered and giggled her way through their art sessions. *Messy, but great fun,* reflected the family pet.

Lara also adored Ben and Sophie's

younger brother but, at four years old, Ollie wasn't quite on the same wavelength. In fact, Ollie was obsessed with computer games and would spend hours killing imaginary baddies. *One day he'll probably make a good secret agent,* thought Lara. *And he loves it when I join in with his shooting games. I always beat him but, no matter, he'll keep on improving. I'm sure Ollie thinks all dogs surf the CBBC website and are good at zapping aliens.*

The Secret Service van drew up in the drive, exactly on time. The usual posse of black-suited agents jumped out and circled the house, eyeing the neighbourhood suspiciously from behind their shades. Everything seemed safe, so Professor Cortex emerged from the vehicle, entering the house without so much as a knock. His two personal bodyguards, Agents T and K, came in with him while another half dozen stood guard outside.

Lara heard them enter the house and reluctantly put the bookmark in her Harry Potter book. She focused on the Professor.

She was a bit annoyed; the book was just getting good.

The professor breezed into the lounge and shook hands with the adults. 'Good morning, Mr and Mrs Cook.' He nodded to Lara. 'Greetings GM451. I trust life as a domestic pet isn't boring you to distraction? Let's get on with things, shall we?'

Always so business-like, thought Lara, thankful that she now belonged to the Cooks. *And, no, life isn't boring, just blissful if you must know.*

'Fine,' agreed Mr Cook. 'Let's do what we have to do,' he sighed, without having any idea of what that was.

Lara nodded in agreement. *The sooner these agents leave the better. I know I used to be part of this outfit but now they just scare me. What on earth will the neighbours think?*

The photographer in the bush tingled with excitement and could hardly breathe, never mind click. The temptation to take more snaps was unbearable, but the special agent standing right by the bush would surely hear his camera if it whirred into action. The house was crawling with men in black, just like the movies. Something big was going on and he and his mate were about to get the exclusive.

Agent P looked nervously all around. He had just drunk a large cup of coffee in the van and needed the toilet. But he was to guard the house – the professor had given him strict instructions not to move away from his post. There was only one thing for it and nobody would notice if he was quick. He looked around and relieved himself in the nearby bush. *Ahhh, the relief.* Then he was back on full alert. Nobody seemed to notice.

Except of course for the newspaper photographer hiding in the shrub. He considered there must be a better way to earn a living. He was now doubly determined to get more evidence of this wonder dog and expose the truth to the world.

The professor nodded to his agents and they began to search the lounge.

'What exactly are they doing?' asked Mum.

'Mr and Mrs Cook,' began the professor in his most serious voice, 'we have reason to believe that GM451 is being stalked. We're not entirely sure by whom. Could be an enemy agent, although it's more likely to be a newspaper reporter.' Lara's ears pricked up. 'We found this at the leisure centre,' he explained, showing Dad a plastic wallet. 'Fake ID. Someone is snooping. And we want to check your house in case you've been bugged.'

Dad laughed. 'You're joking, right?' he said. 'Bugged? No way. Nobody's been in the house except us.' He glanced at Lara, who nodded confidently. *Just me and the custard creams.*

The professor wasn't laughing. He passed the ID badge to Lara, who recognized the photograph at once. *Oh no, the postman,* she thought, slapping her forehead. *How could I have been so stupid?* She trotted over to the mantelpiece and pointed at the card and clock. Professor Cortex picked up the card and read aloud, '"Best wishes from Aunty

Elsie".' He turned to the family and observed them over the top of his spectacles. 'Who's Aunty Elsie?'

Mum and Dad looked blank. 'We haven't got an Aunty Elsie,' said Dad. 'And how long's that clock been there?'

Lara had stopped wagging her tail. *Woops*, she thought. *Looks like I might have made a bit of a mistake.*

One of the men in black took a screwdriver to the clock and removed the back. He gave a thumbs up and pulled out a tiny camera, snapping the wires as he did so.

The professor glared at Lara, who stared at the floor. 'As we suspected. Someone is hot on your tail, GM451. It seems you have become a bit slack. Who knows what kind of data this spy has collected? We must track him down, otherwise your whole identity is at risk. If your special skills become known to the world we will have to take you back undercover and you can kiss goodbye to your family. Understand?'

Ben looked alarmed and Lara nodded solemnly.

'Until we find out more, I am removing

you and your family to a safe place.'

Mum looked horrified. 'What kind of safe place, professor? And for how long?'

'Difficult to say, madam. Could be days, weeks or months. We have to check the area. We would recommend an immediate family holiday until things have cooled down. And I think you should consider some extra protection.'

One of the men in black undid the handcuff from his wrist and laid a suitcase on the floor. He turned the combination lock and clicked it open.

The professor piped up. 'Gadgets, GM451. Gadgets are what you need. James Bond has them but his are a bit gimmicky. After all, he's not actually real, he's just a made-up character, not like you, GM451.' The professor looked around at the concerned faces and carried on. 'I know this looks like a safe neighbourhood and I don't want to spook you, but there is clearly someone tracking you. Therefore I've taken the precaution of issuing you with a couple of pieces of highly technical kit for emergencies.' The professor reached into the case and proudly pulled out two dog collars.

But I've already got one, thought Lara, lifting her head to show off her smart red collar.

'I know you have a collar, GM451, but these special ones incorporate some of the latest spy technology. Let me explain. First of all, this blue one contains a timed electrical device. See this combination? Turn it to ARGH451EEK and in exactly one hundred and twenty seconds the thing will start to give off electric shocks.' He put his spectacles on and fumbled with the combination until there was a beep from the collar. 'There, it's armed. Whoever is in possession of the blue collar one hundred and twenty seconds from now will get a bit tingly. In fact, quite a lot tingly. The collar gives an electric shock strong enough to make your stalker's eyes light up and his fillings fall out, if you know what I mean.' The professor beamed at the gawping audience. He watched as the collar did a very quick pass-the-parcel around the family, nobody wanting to be in possession on the 120th second. 'Electricity is delivered in a pulse. A short burst, then rest, followed by a short burst, then rest. And so on.' The collar came full circle and he smiled at the cleverness of the technology before turning the combination and disarming the device.

Dad sighed with relief. Mum looked horrified.

Ollie was so excited that he couldn't help bouncing up and down. 'Cool. Electric collar. Can I play with it?'

'Certainly not,' snapped Mum. 'Professor, this is a ridiculous thing to put round the neck of a domestic pet. Well, in fact any animal come to think of it. What if it goes off accidentally or someone turns the combination by mistake?'

'My dear lady,' soothed the head of the spy school, 'almost impossible to do. You could give it to your little boy and he could play with the combination all day, all week, in fact all year and he won't come up with ARGH451EEK. The odds are ridiculous. More chance of winning the lottery,' he said, offering the collar to Ollie before Mum snatched it away again. 'But I take your point, madam. It isn't a toy. The effects can be quite long-lasting.' The professor walked over to the window and drew back the net curtain, pointing to one of the men in black patrolling the garden. 'Take Agent E, for example . . . he messed around with the collar and got quite a buzz.'

The family stared at Agent E. His shock of white hair was still standing on end, his eyes were wild and his body occasionally jerked, as if electricity was still crackling through him. Ben imagined that all his fillings must have fallen out.

'Of course, our gadget team has made sure that the technology is perfectly safe,' reassured the professor. 'The collar works out the victim's exact body mass and delivers just the right amount of shock to bring them to submission. The device is triggered by movement. If the victim keeps perfectly still, the collar disarms itself. Perfectly safe.' The professor shot a glance at Agent E, twitching in the garden. 'Like I say, *almost* perfectly safe,' he corrected. 'And it's got one of the latest tracking devices, so we know the collar's whereabouts.'

'And what about the other collar?' enquired Dad, fascinated by the James Bond-style gadgets.

'Oh yes,' said the professor, picking up the black collar. 'This one has a secret compartment containing pills.' The professor reached for his spectacles again. 'Click here and here and this flap opens. See? Inside here are two tiny pills, one green and one pink.' The professor held out the two shiny pills to the wide-eyed family. 'These are designed for emergencies only. They will disable any suspected dognappers or enemy agents. The green one contains a very strong sleeping agent, putting a normal human being into a deep slumber almost instantly. Agent K tested this last week and slept for three days. Isn't that right, Agent K?'

The man in black nodded solemnly, nostrils flaring as he stifled another yawn.

'And the pink one is even better. It contains a powerful drug that will give the swallower severe tummy trouble, making them incapable of anything. Like the sleeping pill, almost instantaneous and very effective –' The professor's mind wandered to Special Agent D who had tested the pink pill some days ago and who had been in the toilet ever since – 'Nasty but very effective indeed.'

'Anything else?' asked Ben excitedly as the professor

returned the pills to their secret compartment on the dog collar.

'We were thinking about issuing GM451 with an automatic pistol like this,' explained the professor, opening Agent T's jacket and showing them his weapon. Mum's eyes grew wide with horror, Ben's with excitement. 'But that's perhaps a bit dangerous in this neighbourhood, especially with kids around.' Mum closed her eyes in relief, Ben and Ollie exchanged glances of disappointment.

'OK, well, I think that's enough gadgets for one day,' said Dad, failing to control his excitement. He turned to Lara. 'Do you want to try on one of your new collars?'

Lara carefully slid her old collar off and placed it on the mantelpiece. She picked up the black one with her paws and clasped it round her neck. *I suppose I ought to show willing*, she thought. *I half hope some baddies do try to get hold of me. If they do they'll be in for the surprise of their lives.*

Professor Cortex snapped his empty case shut and prepared to leave. 'There is one other thing,' he said as he stood in the doorway. 'GM451 has clearly got into some bad habits. She is acting more like a domestic pet than a spy dog and we want to get her skills updated. I think it would be useful if you all visited our top-secret spy school before we send you away for a break.'

Ben and Sophie nodded enthusiastically. Ollie nearly fainted with excitement. Dad's mouth fell open. It was only Mum who wasn't sure.

'It's a brand-new lab, you see,' explained the professor. 'We're very proud of it and I would love to show GM451 our latest developments. Things have moved on in a very short time and she could learn a great deal. Obviously we don't usually open to the public, but GM451 is a special case. She's a bit of a celebrity. In fact, she's more than that.

To our latest trainee spy dogs, she's a legend. I was rather hoping GM451 could give a bit of a talk to our new canine recruits.'

Arrangements were made for the following day and the professor waddled back to his car, an emperor surrounded by his loyal penguins.

The household buzzed with excitement. 'Wow,' said Dad. 'Tomorrow we get to see Lara's top-secret spy school. How exciting's that?'

Lara slunk back to her book, unimpressed by the pending visit. *I don't want to be a celebrity.* She wasn't a spy dog any more – she had carved a much more rewarding role as a family pet. She cringed at her episode with the fake postman. *But I have become a bit careless, so I suppose a skills update won't do any harm.*

The newspaper reporter shushed his colleague with one hand, holding his earpiece in with the other.

His mate watched as a huge grin spread over his face. 'Well,' he mouthed impatiently, 'what are they saying?'

The reporter put his finger to his lips while he listened some more. 'Tomorrow,' he said, rubbing his hands in glee, 'we're going to follow them to spy school.'

5. A Shedload of Adventure

Dad took an early-morning call and noted down everything. This was so secret that there was no address, just a map reference. 'They said we had to bring our wellies,' said Dad with a furrowed brow. 'Doesn't sound very high tech to me.'

The family piled into the people carrier, Lara strapped into the seat in the back. Their journey took them out of the village into the rolling hills of the countryside. They arrived in a small village and Dad pulled up by the side of the road.

'This is it,' Mum announced. 'According to the professor's map coordinates, this is *exactly* where we should be.'

The family strained their necks.

'But there's nothing here,' observed Ben.

'There's a bus shelter, a couple of houses and a phone box, but that's about it.'

'Maybe we should ask someone.' suggested Sophie.

'Oh yeah,' said Ben sarcastically. 'Please, mister, do you know the way to the top-secret spy school? Like the locals would know where it is.'

'Well, do you have any bright ideas?' asked Sophie impatiently.

'Let's take a look,' suggested Dad. 'Maybe there's something obvious that we haven't seen.'

As Dad stepped on to the pavement the telephone in the nearby phone box began to ring. Dad looked puzzled. 'You don't think . . .?' he wondered aloud. Dad strode over to the red phone box and hauled open the door. He picked up the receiver. 'Erm, hello,' he said nervously.

'Good morning, Mr Cook,' crackled a voice at the other end of the phone. 'Congratulations, your map reading is first class.'

'My wife's actually,' replied Dad. 'Who am I speaking to?'

'That doesn't matter,' said the voice. 'Let GM451 out and she will discover the way from here. Bring your wellington boots and make sure nobody's following.' The phone clicked and went dead.

Dad went back to the car with the news. The family burst out in excitement and Lara was pleased to be out in the fresh air. She felt a twinge of excitement too as she put her nose to the ground and sniffed for clues. *Easy-peasy*, she thought, immediately picking up a faint smell of explosives. *Follow me*, she barked as she lolloped off into a nearby field. The Cooks hurried behind, climbing a gate and splodging through the heavy mud. Lara's nose took the family across three muddy fields, their boots getting heavier by the minute. The smell got stronger as Lara galloped across a corn field, past a scarecrow and into a field of cows. She waited while Sophie reclaimed her left wellie from the mud, and then continued towards a small wooden shed, set in the middle of a field, itself in the middle of nowhere.

'Lara,' moaned Ollie, 'are you sure you know what you're doing?'

Lara was equally confused. She recognized the whiff of the professor's home-made brain potion but this was a typical garden shed, with tools hanging up and various plant pots stacked in a corner. To a human it looked perfectly normal, but to Lara's highly sensitive nose it smelt of spy school.

Dad bumbled through the door, followed closely by Ben and Sophie. Eventually Mum and Ollie squeezed inside, the shed now full to bursting.

'Err, Lara,' began Ben, 'you're a bit out of practice. I don't think this is quite what we had in mind. I mean, a few old plant pots and spades are hardly spy-school wizardry,' he said leaning on an old pitchfork.

Before Lara had a chance to bark an explanation, the floor began to sink and the Cooks found themselves descending into a secret underground bunker.

The red Ford had trailed the Cooks' car, keeping a safe distance. The last thing the reporters wanted was to be spotted. But, let's face it, the Cooks hadn't been difficult to follow. Their car was abandoned on a country

43

road and their footprints were clearly pointing the way across a muddy field. The undercover reporters flipped a coin and the loser tucked his trouser bottoms into his socks and slithered his way through the mud. It occasionally got so bad that he disappeared up to his knees, ruining his trainers and trousers, but the man was determined. The family may be on a country walk. Even so, he didn't want to miss a single photo opportunity, especially if it led to somewhere top secret. The tracks took him to a small shed which he approached with extreme caution. He peered through the window. No one there. Just an ordinary shed. He couldn't work it out. The tracks went in but not out, yet the building was empty. He opened the rickety door and entered it. Absolutely nothing. The photographer went back outside and stood awhile, scratching his head. Where on earth can the family have disappeared to? Where exactly is this top-secret spy school?

The lift eventually stopped and the family stepped off it. They watched, aghast, as the shed floor sped back upwards.

'Welcome, my dear friends, welcome,' announced the professor. He was dressed in an all-white jump suit, with white wellington boots and a hairnet protecting his eggshell head. 'Muddy boots off, please,' he said. 'Then you can accompany me into our state-of-the-art spy school.'

The children kicked off their wellies in excitement. Even Lara was impressed. *A tumbledown shed hiding the entrance to the school . . . ingenious, professor,* she thought. Everyone was issued with white cotton socks (even Lara) and they padded quietly behind Professor Cortex. The place was brand new with white clearly the only colour scheme. Tables, chairs, floors, walls, ceilings and computers were all brilliant white. Scientists buzzed around, all dressed in lab coats that looked as if they were from a soap-powder commercial. The professor was clearly proud of his underground school.

'Most of our accelerated education is aimed at dogs,' he explained. 'GM451 has shown us what's possible, so we've given up on rats, cats and monkeys – either totally untrainable or completely thick.'

Ben peered through a round window and saw several pigs in a gym. Some were trotting on treadmills, while others were practising sit-ups; all were sweating, like pigs do.

'Pigs have serious potential,' said the professor. 'Highly intelligent but not very athletic. This experiment is designed to test whether we can produce a super-fit pig that can cover vast distances with ease.'

'And?' enquired Ben. 'Is it possible?'

'Not so far, young fellow,' sighed the professor. He took some chalk and scribbled a maths formula on a nearby board. 'If X represents food intake, Y is exercise and Z is speed, then this seems to be happening,' he said, scribbling some more. 'And we weren't expecting it,' he muttered, deep in thought.

Puzzled faces squinted at the complicated series of letters and graphs on the board.

'Right,' nodded Dad. 'And what does that all mean?'

'Oh, very simple, really, dear chap. Exercising pigs just seems to build their appetite. The food bill has gone through

the roof, yet they're still as slow as ever.'

'Why didn't he just say that?' hissed Sophie as the professor marched them off down the next brilliant white corridor. 'I think he's bonkers.'

They stopped at a huge white door and the professor placed his hand on a glass plate. The plate lit up and Professor Cortex stood still while a white light scanned over his face, recording the detail of his eyes. The door slid open and the family followed him into a large lecture theatre, with a class in full swing. Two white-suited women were beaming some sums on to a big screen and the student dogs were expected to tap their answers into their laptops. Lara remembered doing something similar when she had been at spy school.

'Three plus five?' asked one of the women.

The dogs solemnly tapped away at their computers. Lara wandered among them. One or two got it right, but most hadn't a clue.

'And, finally, six plus ten?' said the other woman. 'Let's show the professor how clever you are. One of you bark the right answer.'

The dogs looked at each other. *Six plus ten? What on earth is the teacher going on about?* They looked at their top dog, who cleared his throat and barked four times. The dog students looked hopefully at the teachers, one of whom shook her head, the other clasping her forehead in dismay.

'They still have some way to go,' whispered the professor from behind his hand. He decided it was time to step in. 'Veronica, Sylvia and dogs of spy school, may I interrupt your maths class and welcome some very special guests. To my left are Mr and Mrs Cook and their three children. This is the family you have read about in the school magazine. They kindly adopted our first-ever Licensed Assault and Rescue Animal, GM451, and have looked after her ever since.'

The family nodded modestly, except Ollie who waved enthusiastically. The dogs responded by wagging their tails hard. They had no idea what the professor was saying but he was a nice man who sometimes gave them treats.

'And to my left is GM451, the world's first super dog. Our first graduate of this programme. A dog that has gone well beyond any other. A dog that should be an inspiration for you all. I'm hoping that GM451 will say a few words to you.'

The professor beckoned Lara forward. She approached the laptop at the front of the class and, using a pencil in her mouth, logged on to the Internet. She opened a news page and headlines from around the world appeared on the big screen. The headlines screamed of crime, terror and disasters. What followed sounded like a series of barks, woofs and whines, but it was actually a doggie speech with Lara wishing all the dogs well in their forthcoming spy training. *You are probably not aware of the terrible things going on in the world*, she barked, pointing her paw at the screen behind her. *But you have the chance to get involved in doing good for our government, solving crimes and catching criminals.* She was pleased that the trainees were sitting up straight and listening. Most were wagging their tails enthusiastically. *It's dangerous but very worthwhile work. Listen to the professor and his team. They will teach you well.* After she'd finished, the dogs finally understood the importance of their training. They howled their approval and vowed to do their very best for the professor and their country. Veronica and Sylvia continued the maths lesson, pleased at the dogs' new enthusiasm for learning. One day, if they were to save the world, they might need to know six plus ten.

As they turned to leave, one of the professor's team approached and thrust a piece of paper into his hand. 'It's a possible T5, sir,' explained the agent, looking a little worried.

The professor raised an eyebrow. 'A T5? How close?'

'Very, sir. Entered the shed and had a look round. Carrying a camera, sir.'

The professor looked concerned. 'Please follow me,' he said to the puzzled faces. The family and Lara were led to a small room with a huge flat-screen monitor.

'T5 visual, please,' snapped the professor and the screen sprang into life. The Cooks watched footage of a man with a camera struggling through the mud and into the shed. As he left the shed the video zoomed on to his face and the picture froze in close-up. Lara immediately recognized him as the pretend postman. 'We have various security cameras at ground level. This one is hidden in a scarecrow and I think it's captured our spy,' explained the professor. 'Do you recognize this man?' he said, suddenly very serious.

Heads nodded unanimously. 'It's the face of the man on the ID card at the leisure centre,' noted Ben.

'And probably the fake postman too,' added Mum.

Lara was avoiding eye contact.

The professor turned to his aide. 'Does

he show up on any face recognition?'

'Negative, sir,' replied the agent sharply. 'He's clean. Well, very muddy actually, but clean as far as our records go. Never shown up before.'

'And the camera?'

'Unlikely to be a birdwatcher, sir. Do you want us to pick him up?'

The professor nodded. 'Take him in for questioning. I want to know everything about this man – name, age, background, inside leg measurement and especially why he's tracking GM451.'

Lara and the Cooks continued their tour of the spy school. They got to meet members of G-Team, whose job was to develop the latest animal spy gadgets and gizmos.

'Come on in and take a look,' enthused one of the white-overalled scientists, all of whom seemed to know Lara. 'Get a load of this, GM451,' he said excitedly, taking a package from his pocket. 'Exploding dog biscuits. They look and taste exactly like doggie treats, except I wouldn't recommend you eat one. Watch this.' He marched to the other end of the room and pushed a doggie treat into the soil of a plant pot. 'Perfectly safe until you add water.' He poured a few drops from a watering can before retreating back to the family. 'Fingers in ears,' he demonstrated, and, seconds later, the pot exploded with a dull thud, spraying soil across the room.

'Now that's pretty cool,' said Ben dusting himself off. 'Can I have some to take to school?' he asked, thinking of all the practical jokes he could play.

'Far too dangerous, dear chap. But you can take some of these,' said the technical expert, handing him a box of dog biscuits. 'They look and taste exactly like normal dog biscuits. And do you know why?' Ben shook his head. The inventor smiled at the array of blank faces. 'Because they *are* normal dog biscuits, that's why!' he beamed, biting into one and grimacing. 'Err, liver and onions.'

'So why are they for spies?' asked Ben

'Because, Mr Questions, they all have letters on, that's why. Like M&Ms, except

M&Ms only have Ms. What's the point of that, I ask you? Our dog biscuits have all the letters, like Scrabble.' The faces were still blank, so the scientist pressed on. 'Take GM451, for example,' he said, patting Lara's head. 'We plant her in a criminal's hideout to do some spying. She acts as a normal household pet and becomes part of the gang. When they feed her, she simply leaves coded messages for us, spelled out in dog biscuits. Simple or what? All the best tricks are entirely simple.'

Professor Cortex thanked G-Team for their time and moved the family on. Their final stop was a room with a huge window

MI5
INTERVIEW
IN PROGRESS

through which they could see the captured spy, sitting at a table.

'Here's our T5,' pointed the professor. 'He's been secured in the interview room – can't see us but we can see him. He's already been questioned.' Professor Cortex fixed his glasses on to the end of his nose and looked down at his notes. 'Claims to be a newspaper reporter. Working alone. He says he was going to sell his pictures to the highest bidder,' he read, raising his eyes above his glasses to gauge reactions. 'No weapon, unless you count his camera. We've processed his film and found these.'

Half a dozen photos were passed around.

Lara smiled at the picture of her scoring the winning goal at the leisure centre. *It wasn't a bad volley, was it?* she thought, puffing out her chest.

'We will hold him here for further questioning,' added the professor. 'By the time he gets out – if he gets out – you will be safely on holiday. I will call GM451 in the morning to arrange the details.' He looked Lara in the eye. 'Please be careful, GM451. Stay alert and take no chances. There may be others tracking you.'

Lara nodded solemnly. *OK, prof. No more mistakes. I will guard myself and my family to the very best of my ability.*

They shook hands with Professor Cortex, who gave them a large bag containing their wellies. 'You shouldn't need these at the top.' He smiled as the lift doors closed. They looked at each other in puzzlement as the lift sped to the surface. Eventually the doors swished open and the family found themselves in the bus shelter across the road from their car.

'What . . .? How . . .?' exclaimed Dad.

Lara was very impressed as she padded

across the road in her white socks. *I think I look rather good in these*, she thought as she jumped into the back seat.

The reporter in the red car agreed. He was parked some way down the road and his zoom lens whirred into action, catching the white-socked dog trotting across the road. He had seen the family emerging from the bus shelter, but couldn't remember there being a bus. 'Disappearing into a shed and then reappearing out of a bus stop,' he muttered aloud. 'All with white socks on, even the dog . . . this family gets stranger by the minute,' he murmured as the shutter clicked greedily

6. Holiday Orders

The following day Lara answered an early-morning call from the professor. Ben watched her nodding into the mobile, scribbling notes as she listened.

'So, GM451, it will be a holiday of sorts. It seems sensible for you to work on a mission while you're away. Nothing too dangerous, of course, but I don't want the family to know. This is top secret, just like the old days. Unfold your map and look at square FF54.'

Ben watched as Lara struggled to unfold the map and lay it out on the kitchen table. She ran her paw over it, obviously looking for somewhere specific.

'The two towns in this area have had a spate of dognappings,' explained the professor.

'It seems as though a gang is operating, stealing pedigree dogs and selling them in London. Sometimes they are even being returned to their original owners, in exchange for a big, fat reward. We think it's part of an international dog-smuggling ring. Someone is making a fortune, GM451. More than sixty dogs have disappeared in the last two months.'

Lara let out a soft whistle. *That's a lot of unhappy owners*, she thought.

The professor continued, even more serious than before. 'Personally, I can't think of anyone better qualified than our number-one spy dog to solve this canine crime. Seeing as these towns are by the sea, I think you could combine the family holiday with a bit of mystery-solving. What do you say, GM451? Two barks if you're in.'

There was silence as Lara considered the options. *I'm retired from spying*, she thought. *I could just go on holiday and relax. But I suppose this is pretty safe for the family. After all, dognappers aren't going to be interested in the children. And I would be helping out my own species.*

Ben listened as Lara barked twice down

the phone. She turned to him, with a glint in her eye. *Looks like adventure beckons.*

The holiday was hastily arranged. Ben had persuaded Mum and Dad to let the children go camping. 'We can use my new tent,' he'd pleaded, 'and Lara will keep us safe.' Mum wasn't the outdoor sort, so she'd agreed to let the children camp, so long as they took their older cousins, Hayley and Adam. Mum, Dad and Ollie would stay in a bed and breakfast nearby.

Ben and Sophie were very excited. Hayley would be great fun. Adam was a bit of a wimp but they could stomach him for a few days, and Lara would be a much more exciting camping companion than Ollie.

The Cooks set off for the coast, where they were to meet up with Hayley and Adam. They drove into dognapper territory and Lara immediately noticed the lack of dogs. *Weird,* she thought. *And look how many houses have got lost dog posters in the window.*

Dad pulled up at the bed and breakfast, a beautiful pub close to the coast and the moors. Ben, Sophie and Ollie rushed in to meet their cousins while Mum and Dad unpacked the car. Lara sniffed around the car park, noticing yet another 'Lost Dog' notice on the gate. She studied the picture of the poodle, marvelling at the stupid name. *Princess Teensie*, she cringed. *How can you do that to a dog? But look at the size of the reward. The owners must be desperate to get her back. I'll see if I can solve this mystery and get your princess back.*

Lara nosed her way into the pub and was pleased to see the children all getting along nicely. Hayley was tall, slim and blonde; a very sporty young lady who naturally excelled at everything. She lived in a big city and was much more street-wise than her cousins. In many respects, Adam was the exact opposite of his sister. He was ultra sensible, carrying a first-aid kit with him at all times. He hated getting dirty and liked everything to be organized. As the school swot, he felt compelled to comb his hair sideways. He wasn't too keen on camping, noting the potential hazards: they might get lost on the moors, drown in the sea, fall off a cliff, get sunburnt, get captured by pirates . . . Hayley cut him off mid-sentence, convincing him that Lara would help keep them safe. She couldn't help adding, 'Besides, occasionally it's good to do something a bit risky. And if there are pirates, we might have a bit of an adventure.' The children were wide-eyed, Hayley in anticipation and her brother in fear.

The family had an evening meal at the pub before Hayley and Adam's dad said his farewells. It was too late to camp that evening so everyone settled down for a night indoors. Lara eyed the pub customers suspiciously. *One of you could be a dognapper*, she thought. *Or one of you could be a baddie spy, tracking me.* She was secretly very excited.

She sniffed a few customers and listened in on several conversations. She approached two shabbily dressed men in the corner and was overpowered by the smell of dogs. The big man patted her head and threw her some chips.

'Hello, poochy,' said his friend. 'Do you want to join our merry gang?'

Merry gang? thought Lara.

'Our merry gang of stolen pooches,' laughed the half-drunk man.

'N . . . n . . . not a pedigree,' said the big man offering Lara an onion ring.

'And far too ugly to sell,' smirked his friend. 'And he's even got a hole in his ear.'

I beg your pardon, thought Lara. *I'm a she. And what do you mean, too ugly? You're no oil painting yourself, mate. And I got this hole protecting my family,* Lara thought proudly. *Looks like I may have already found the dognappers. I think all I have to do is follow you to find my dognapped friends. I could have this mystery solved by midnight.*

She watched as the men scraped the remains of their meal into a bag. *Probably to feed the captured dogs.* She was about to follow them out of the door when she was called by Ben.

'Bed time, Lara,' he shouted.

But I've got some dognappers to follow . . . a crime to solve . . . some dogs to rescue . . . a mission to complete. She glanced at the clock. *And it's only ten o'clock. James Bond doesn't have to be in bed by ten, does he now?*

But Dad already had her by the collar. 'Come on, super dog,' he said, smiling at the dognappers. 'Give these poor men a rest and we can get some sleep. Tomorrow you are taking the kids camping, so you need your beauty sleep.'

That night, as the family slept comfortably, Lara lay wide-eyed and restless. She'd let the dog smugglers get away, but that wasn't what was keeping her awake. *First the men said I was too ugly to be dognapped, and then Dad said I needed 'beauty sleep'. These humans certainly know how to hurt a girl's feelings.*

★

Outside, the photographer in the red Ford shuffled uncomfortably. He was being extra careful now that his colleague had been captured by the Secret Service. He had his front seat back as far as it would go, but he still fidgeted and was dreadfully cold. He had followed the Cooks all the way from the Midlands, keeping a safe distance, of course. He had watched the last light in the pub go out and decided that nothing else would happen tonight. But the journey had been worthwhile. Earlier in the evening he'd snapped some pictures of the mutt playing pool; pretty good she was too, winning a black-ball game. Tomorrow he intended to get more pictures, ones that would prove beyond doubt that this was a super dog. These would be the pictures that made his fortune. The discomfort and cold would be worth it.

7. *Surf's Up*

The following day all the children were up bright and early, tucking into a hearty full English breakfast. Dad checked through their camping gear and helped pack their rucksacks. Maps were studied and the route traced one last time. Mum and Dad were to drop the four older children and Lara off at a nearby seaside town. After staying on a local campsite, they would move on to the moors for another couple of nights before making their way back to the B&B. They had all the essentials for a camping holiday: map, food, mobile phone, sleeping bags, tent, water, matches, torches and a pack of cards (for when it rained). Adam checked everything against his alphabetical tick list and then checked again.

Dad had a long private word with Lara before they left. 'We are trusting you with the safety of the children,' he lectured, rather too sternly for Lara's liking. 'We want you to treat this as seriously as you would one of your missions, OK?'

Lara nodded solemnly, stifling a yawn. *Blimey, you make it sound as if it's a top-secret trip into enemy territory! Chill out a bit. It's a three-night camping holiday by the seaside,* she thought. *What danger could there possibly be? The kids will have a great time and I'll see if I can smash the dog-smuggling ring while I'm at it.*

'So stay alert,' Dad continued, wagging his finger. 'The children are to be polite, sensible and well behaved. There's to be no talking to strangers and no noise on the campsite after ten o'clock. And absolutely no silly behaviour at any time.'

Lara rolled her eyes. *It's a holiday. It's meant to be 100 per cent silly behaviour,* she thought.

'Have we got a deal?' Dad asked, holding out his hand.

Lara sighed. *Deal,* she nodded, shaking on it. *But I might have to bend your rules just a teeny bit, otherwise we'll have no fun at all.*

On the first day Lara hardly had to bend the rules at all. They all helped pitch the tent and then it was wall-to-wall fun. The children revelled in their independence, unable to believe they were responsible for themselves, with no parents to answer to. Mum phoned six times, just to check everything was all right.

Towards the end of their day at the seaside it was decided that they would have a go at surfing. After all, lots of locals seemed to be out there making it look very easy. Even Adam was keen. Lara was desperate to be included as it wasn't something she'd tried before but looked great fun. When the children entered the surf hire shop she barked at Sophie. To Sophie it sounded like 'Woof, woof, bark, whine,' but it actually meant, '*If you lot are going surfing, can I come too?*' Hayley jokingly suggested that Lara might want to come surfing with them. Everyone laughed. The cousins had heard of Lara's special abilities and, after watching her play pool, they were really looking forward to seeing what other skills she had, but surfing was stretching their imaginations.

Lara couldn't believe she was being ridiculed. *Why shouldn't I go surfing? If humans can do it, then so can I.* She had to get her point across before it was too late. Lara stood on her hindlegs and gently slid one of the surfboards from the display on to the ground. Then she stood on it – surfer-style – legs apart, bent at the knees, paws out to keep balance. She gave a half bark to attract Adam's attention. He turned round, eyes wide in amazement, to see Lara demonstrating her surfing technique. *See, I really do want to have a go at surfing.*

An extra surfboard was hired, Hayley explaining to the assistant that they had another friend waiting down at the beach. 'Well, I could hardly tell him it was for the dog, could I?' she explained. The children had agreed that they would have to keep Lara's surfing exploits secret. Ben had explained that Lara had promised not to draw attention to herself in case people started making a fuss. 'Just be a normal dog,' Professor

Cortex had advised. 'That's the safest option.'

The children now faced a long walk. If Lara was to join them in the waves they had to find a secluded bit of cove where nobody could see them. Front-page headlines screaming 'Canine Surf Dude' would hardly be blending into the background. The children hauled their surfboards and wetsuits a mile along the beach, past lots of normal dogs chasing sticks and frisbees. Ben smiled to himself: his dog couldn't just catch frisbees, she could throw them too.

Eventually the children reached the far end of the beach, deserted of holidaymakers who didn't want to walk too far for an ice cream. But it was perfect for Lara to try her paw at surfing. The conditions were ideal, a rough sea throwing up good surf and the perfect setting, with golden sand backed by steep cliffs. Ben, Sophie, Adam and Hayley squeezed into their wetsuits and then the children and Lara raced into the waves with their boards. They were all expert swimmers and spent the next two hours clowning about in the water, toppling off waves and generally exhausting themselves. Surfing was a lot harder than it looked. Hayley just about managed to mount her surfboard once, while her brother and cousins failed dismally. Lara was the only one to get the hang of it and she gleefully rode several waves, howling with delight and punching the air every time. *What a holiday! What a triumph! What an achievement for the canine species!* The children and surf dog eventually waded from the water, high fived and collapsed on the sand.

'You, Lara, are the weirdest, best, most talented, funniest dog in the whole world,' shouted Hayley above the noise of the

waves. Lara lay spreadeagled on the sand and looked up at the blue sky. She considered this to be the best day of her life.

She didn't notice the man on the cliff who was also having the best day of his life. For one thing, he'd remembered his telephoto lens, enabling him to clearly pick out the surfers below. He couldn't help talking out loud to himself. 'My, my, my. First she plays football, then cycles, then wears socks, then plays pool and now she surfs. I think we should share this mutt's talents with the whole world.' He lay flat on his stomach, perched on the edge of the cliff, clicking away. He took several shots of the children grappling with their wetsuits before training his lens on the surfing dog. He was struggling to grasp the magnitude of the story and was salivating at the thought of the money his pictures would fetch. Perhaps he should auction them to the highest bidder. He wondered if a million was too much to ask. 'It's a shame my mate isn't here to share this good fortune.' He smiled as he changed the film and gorged himself on more pictures.

8. Camping on Spindle Island

Early next morning the children and Lara packed up and ventured on to the wilderness of the moors. They had a slap-up breakfast in a seaside cafe to build up their energy reserves for what promised to be an exciting day of hiking and camping. Hayley was in charge of the map and led the way, Lara lolloping alongside, sniffing for rabbits. The children's route didn't take them too far away from the seaside village, just up on to the moors and a few miles along the coast. The map indicated a remote picnic area which was to be the campsite for the next two evenings.

'Just think, tonight we'll be camping in the wild,' enthused Ben as they walked along the coast path. 'Nobody for miles around. What an adventure.'

'And we can visit Spindle Island,' said Sophie. 'If we wait until low tide we can walk to it and explore the caves. Remember what Dad said though, Hayley. We must time it right or we'll get cut off by the tide and have to spend the night there.'

Adam started to complain about the dangers of exploring caves, but his words fell on ears deafened by excitement.

'Why don't we camp there?' suggested a wide-eyed Hayley. 'All we have to do is find a flat spot and pitch the tent. When the tide comes in we'll be surrounded by sea and it will feel like our own proper island.'

Lara listened, taking it all in. She wasn't sure about camping on Spindle Island. From what she had seen of the map it wasn't actually an island at all, just a headland that was cut off by the sea at high tide. Lara could see that the children were excited at the prospect of making their own decisions. She decided to go with the flow – if they wanted to set up camp on the headland, then so be it. She decided it wasn't any more dangerous than camping on the moors – they would just have to time the tides right, that's all.

The children continued their hike, marching along at quite a pace, spurred on by the excitement of pitching their tent all alone on Spindle Island. Adam had threatened to turn back but the others had talked him round. Lara went ahead to check the site, sniffing as she ran. At one point Hayley took the wrong path and Lara had to stand on her hindlegs and whistle to the children, beckoning them the right way. By noon they had made it to Spindle Island. It was about the size of a school playing field and joined to the mainland by a short stretch of rocks. The tide was low, so they dashed along the rocks to the headland and devoured a hearty picnic, watching as the sea gradually covered the rocks. Ben, Hayley and Lara took charge of the tent, while Sophie and Adam collected firewood. Once the camp was sorted, the children set off down a steep path to the far end of the headland, where the sea was pounding the cliffs. They knew there were caves along the headland and vowed to explore them at low tide. For now, they just watched and marvelled at the force of the ocean.

As always happens on a camping holiday, dark clouds gathered and rain set in. Lara and the children retreated into the tent and played cards while the rain pelted down, making a terrific noise. Despite the awful weather the children felt comfortable and safe as they snuggled down into the warmth of their sleeping bags. By eight o'clock they were all sound asleep.

Lara woke at midnight. Something wasn't quite right. The rain was still lashing down and making a terrific racket on the tent, but her superb doggie ears picked up another noise. It sounded like barking, but it couldn't be; they were miles from anywhere. She squirmed further into her sleeping bag and tried to ignore it – she wasn't a spy dog any more, she was normal. *Stop investigating every sight and sound. It's probably nothing . . . most likely my imagination . . . but what if it is something? Could be a boat getting too close to the shore. Could be a dog in trouble. Could be . . .* She had to investigate. It was bred into her.

Lara carefully nosed out of the tent and stumbled into the dark and gusty blackness.

The rain poured down. *Was this such a good idea? Perhaps I should just crawl back into my sleeping bag, put my paws in my ears and pretend nothing's going on. But no, there it was again. Shouting. And barking. Who on earth could be out at this hour in this location?* It was coming from the seaward end of the island, so Lara headed towards the cliff to have a look. She reached the cliff edge and looked out to sea, squinting in the rain. There was a sheer drop below her and the sea was relentlessly crashing against the cliffs. Although the vast expanse of ocean was black, she could see the white of the foam as the waves pounded the rocks below. A few hundred metres from shore was a light. *It must be a boat. Why is it out at night? Most peculiar.* Lara stood and watched for a few minutes. The boat was moving slowly, probably being rowed, but she couldn't be sure. There was just a single light on board, perhaps a torch. When the wind was in the right direction Lara could hear an occasional shout from the boat. It was gradually coming closer to the shore. The pitch blackness meant she couldn't make out much detail, but the boat was definitely coming ashore. She watched it approach the headland and then disappear under her. *Must be into a cave*, she thought. *Where else could it have gone? But who's landing in a remote cave at this ridiculous hour in this disgusting weather?*

The rain continued to thunder down and the waves threw themselves against the rocks, but the people had gone, so she began to lose interest. She was just about to give up and go back to her sleeping bag when she heard more voices. Two men were climbing the steep path

from the beach below, one shining a torch, the other stumbling behind.

'Will you keep that light steady, idiot!' yelled the one at the rear. 'I nearly fell to me death.'

'Sorry,' came the reply. 'I . . . I . . .'

'I know, I'm sorry, mate. I didn't mean it. Won't happen again. Am I right?'

Lara recognized them by their smell. It was the men from the pub, the suspected dognappers. She lay low as they passed, then followed discreetly, trying to listen in on their conversation. She sprinted from one clump of bracken to the next, glad of the cover of darkness. This was like spying and her adrenalin was pumping again. She caught another snippet of conversation as the men made their way across the narrow rocky causeway of land that had emerged at low tide.

'We'll finish the job tomorrow, right, Ned?'

'R . . . R . . . R . . .' revved the big man, trying desperately to form his words.

'For goodness' sake, spit it out, idiot. What you meant to say is, "Righto, Bill, we'll pop back tomorrow and pick up the smuggled dogs, load 'em in the lorry and be in London by Thursday evening." Am I right?'

He wasn't. What Ned wanted to say was, 'Wrong. I'm sick of this whole game. I want out. Forget the smuggling and forget the money. We're in this up to our necks, so let's just scarper.'

Lara was now on red alert. She had heard Bill's words and her spy-dog training came rushing back to her. She considered what to do. Her first priority had to be the children. She had promised Dad that they would come to no harm, so she had to protect them. The best course of action was to follow the dognappers, then return to the tent and try and let the children know what was going on. Hayley could telephone the police and all would be fine. *That is the simplest solution and poses the lowest risk,* she thought logically.

Lara followed Ned and Bill back to the mainland, where they took refuge in a tumbledown house on a disused farm. She approached it and was met by a snarling, aggressive Dobermann dog, tied to a rope, thankfully. It rushed at Lara in a frenzy of anger, nearly throttling itself when it reached the end of the rope. *Ah, aggressive and very stupid. I've met your sort before.* The men heard their dog barking and came to investigate, shining a torch into the trees.

'What is it, Max? What is it, boy?' shouted Bill.

'Might be a r . . . r . . . r . . .' began Ned.

'Might be a rabbit, I know, mate, probably is. Let's have a drink, get some kip and see what tomorrow brings,' interpreted Bill.

What Ned had wanted to say was, 'Might be a raid. It could be the police coming to get us. Let's just call it a day. I can't stand another night sleeping on the floor in this godforsaken shack. Prison would be better than this.'

Max eventually went back to sleep and Lara crept from her hiding place and sneaked over to a window to see if she could catch a glimpse of the smugglers. She jumped up and put her paws on the window sill, peeping in through the broken glass. Inside the farmhouse were dozens of cages, housing dogs of all shapes and sizes. She looked at their sad eyes.

Wow, I've not seen anything like this since I booked in at the RSPCA, Lara thought. *I've got to find a way to rescue these poor mutts and get them back to their owners.* She took a good look at the men, who were trying to get comfortable by a small fire. The stutterer was a large, lean man with a big forehead and sad eyes set in a long face. *If owners look like their dogs, he must have a bloodhound,* she thought. Bill was sitting closer to the flickering fire, so he was easier to make out. He was smaller, podgier, with currant eyes set in a piggy face. *More of a pit bull terrier.* Lara could make out tattoos on his neck and hands. She strained to read them. His

neck had a dotted line with 'Cut Here' written along it. Bill's knuckles had what looked like 'LEFT' and 'RITE' tattooed on them. *Even his spelling is terrible*, she thought. Both men were soaking wet. They wore thick coats, woolly hats and fingerless gloves. Lara sniffed through the hole in the glass and could tell they'd not seen a bar of soap for a very long time.

'Best get some shut-eye,' said Bill. 'Tomorrow we need to get down to the cave and pick up the last batch of hounds.' He scrunched himself into a ball to try and get warm, while Ned just sat and stared into space, rubbing his stubbly chin.

Lara's sticky-up ear stood to attention. *What? Oh no, not the cave. Not the cave that the kids are planning to visit. What on earth am I going to do?* She remembered her promise to Dad and her mind ran wild with the various options, none of which seemed very appealing. *These two are bedding down for the night,* she thought. *There's not much I can do here, so I'd better try and get some rest myself. And tomorrow I've got to find a way of keeping the children safe from the smugglers.* Lara tiptoed past the snoring Max and then sprinted back to the island, swimming across the sea-covered causeway.

Lara returned to the tent, her mind trying to formulate a plan. She gave herself a good shake before carefully stepping into the tent and climbing back into her sleeping bag. Her mind was racing, so sleep was impossible. She lay awake listening to Adam snore, considering what daybreak would bring.

9. Some Serious Juggling

Everyone woke at first light – you always do when you're camping. The rain had stopped but the landscape was soaked.

'Did everyone sleep well?' croaked Hayley, hair everywhere and a zigzag pattern on her face where she'd been lying face down on her sleeping-bag zip. 'Looks like it might have rained a bit in the night,' she observed, peeping out of the tent flap.

A bit! thought Lara. *It's all right for some, but I was out in it most of the night, thank you very much. And it wasn't a bit, it was a lot. And as for sleeping well . . . what with the noise of the rain, finding the dog smugglers and Adam's snoring, personally I didn't sleep a wink.* She thought about Bill and Ned, who were probably on their way towards the cave right now. *And now I've got to find the safest way to get everyone back home and contact the police to catch the smugglers. I think the first thing is to stop you lot exploring the cave. I certainly don't want you bumping into the smugglers down there. But how am I going to communicate? Think, Lara, think.*

'Did you sleep well, Lara?' asked Sophie, affectionately cuddling her dog.

Now's my chance. Lara shook her head, trying to look as solemn as she could. She stabbed a paw in the direction of outside and tried to pull a baddie face.

'What, you didn't sleep well because you wanted to sleep outside?' said Ben. 'Of course, here you are cooped up with us when you would have preferred to sleep out in the open.'

'Too dangerous out there,' warned Adam.

'Well, tonight you can sleep outside,' offered Ben, ignoring his cousin's concerns. 'It'll give us all a bit more room in here.'

Err, that's not exactly what I meant, thought Lara. She shook her head again. *How do I get my message across?* She had an idea. She rummaged in a rucksack and pulled out her alphabet dog biscuits. *Perfect*, she thought. *I can spell 'smugglers' and everyone will understand.* Lara beckoned the children outside. She stood on her hindlegs and had a good look towards the mainland to see if the smugglers were coming. There was no sign yet, so she scattered the biscuits on to the ground. *Quick, Lara, quick.* She turned them all over and started searching for the correct letters. The children watched, puzzled.

'I can't believe you're so hungry,' said Hayley.

'I don't think she's going to eat them, I think she's trying to spell something, aren't you, Lara?' encouraged Ben. 'They're spy biscuits that we got from the professor. Are you trying to tell us something?'

Lara nodded solemnly. She hunted frantically for the other letters. *I can find an S and M but where's the U and G?* she thought, frantically turning the biscuits on to their letter sides. *Too many X, Y and Zs. I can spell 'xylophone' but not 'smuggler'.* All she could find from 'smuggler' was the 'S', 'M' and a half-eaten 'E'. *Mmm, I need another plan.* Lara wrinkled her forehead as she thought hard.

Got it. She put her paw up in front of Ben's face as if to say 'Wait'. Lara bounded across the moor and collected three small rocks. She returned a minute later and the children gathered round, curious.

'Go on, Lara, do your stuff,' encouraged Ben proudly. 'She's a spy dog, see. What did I tell you?'

OK, here goes, thought the pet. She had seen humans play mime games and decided this was her best chance. She laid the 'S' and 'M' out before the children. *OK, guys. It begins with 'SM'. And this is the rest.* She picked up the rocks and began to juggle, figuring they would soon guess that 'juggler' rhymed with 'smuggler'. She fumbled the first rock and it fell on her paw. *Ow, that hurt a lot.* She hopped around a little while the girls giggled

and the boys just stared, a bit bewildered.

'Looks a bit dangerous to me,' observed Adam. 'Do you need a plaster?'

Lara ignored him and tried again. She'd seen clowns in the movies and was sure she could do it. She picked the rocks up and began to toss them into the air, this time more successfully. *Great.* She got into a rhythm and her confidence grew. She did a bit of a jig while she juggled the three rocks, then threw them high into the air, twizzled and let them drop at her feet before curtsying and blowing kisses to the audience. *Not bad for a beginner!*

The children clapped enthusiastically. 'Great juggling, Lara,' smiled Ben.

Lara barked and shook her head. *Come on, guys, get your thinking caps on. Look at the S and M, put it with juggler and what have you got?*

'You want *us* to juggle?' guessed Adam.

Lara held her head in her paws. *For goodness' sake. 'Juggler' rhymes with 'smuggler', can't you see? Don't you get it?* Lara pointed frantically to the alphabet biscuits. *'SM' and 'juggler' makes 'smuggler' Go on, say it. Smuggler. Smuggler. SMUG . . . ULL . . . ERR,* she willed.

' "Juggling" and "SM",' thought Adam aloud. 'It just doesn't make sense.'

Heaven help me, thought Lara, smacking her paw against her forehead in desperation. *The 'SM' goes at the front, instead of the 'J'. It's obvious, isn't it? A baddie who hides things in a cave isn't a juggler, now is he?*

Hayley's mind was elsewhere. 'Can we do this juggling thing later?' she said. 'I want to go and explore the caves. Look, the tide is low, so now is a great time. Anyone coming?'

Uh oh. That's exactly where I don't want you to go, panicked Lara. The dog shook her head gravely, wagging her paw like Mum sometimes wagged her finger, trying to make her point. *Do not go anywhere near those caves. Got it? Caves equal danger.*

'Oh, OK, if you want to be a boring old misery guts you can stay here and finish your Harry Potter book, I suppose,' said Hayley to the family pet. 'We're off to explore.'

Nightmare. Lara reached for the rocks again and began to juggle. *Maybe one more try?* She put on a silly doggie smile and a bit more of a show. *Please don't go to the caves, there may be baddies down there; if not now, later. If you don't get the smuggler rhyme, then please just stay here and watch me juggle. Look, I'm a juggling dog – clever, eh?* As she juggled she smiled, rolled her eyes, pulled faces and stuck her tongue out. *Just stay and watch me. Please don't go!* She juggled desperately, as if her life depended on it. For all she knew, it probably did.

The problem with being a spy dog with special skills is that eventually your family comes to take you for granted. If any other dog in the world had stood on its hindlegs and juggled three rocks, everyone would have been in shock but, because it was Lara, they brushed it aside. 'Come on, get your trainers on, we're going for an adventure,' said Hayley.

The lone photographer had not slept well for two nights. His small tent had become waterlogged and he was soaked to the skin. His teeth chattered and his nose had a permanent dewdrop. His colleague had been captured, so it was down to him to get the necessary pictures. From this range he could just about pick out the tent and the children. He was too far away to hear but he was observing them magnified through his telephoto lens – like watching a silent movie. The dog was juggling – click, click, click – the night had been hell but the day was heaven. He held his hands steady to get the best shot he could. 'This one is for my mate,' he growled through chattering teeth.

10. Into the Smugglers' Cave

Ned and Bill woke with bad headaches. They surfaced slowly. Ned made a small fire to try and warm the farmhouse up. Bill couldn't stand the yapping dogs, so he opened the door and stumbled out into the semi-darkness. He let Max off for a run, watching proudly as his dog thundered after a rabbit. Since his mind was elsewhere, he didn't notice the beauty of the landscape as the sun rose over the horizon.

'Today's the day,' said Bill, finding Ned staring into the flames.

'Y . . . Y . . . Y . . .' He stopped and composed himself. He tried to stay calm and focus on the sentence he wanted to say: you go alone. I want to go back to town, get a job, try going straight. I don't want to be part of this any more. You take my share of the money. Just let me back out, please. Ned focused. He couldn't get past the first word. 'Y . . . Y . . . Y . . .'

Bill stepped in again, incorrectly second-guessing his colleague's sentence. 'Yes, I'm ready to go. Let's hike across to the island, collect the rest of the dogs and get them loaded into the lorry. C'mon, let's go.'

Ned spluttered into voice again. 'R . . . R . . .'

'Right, mate,' echoed Bill.

What Ned wanted to say was not 'right', but 'wrong': 'What we're doing is wrong. Smuggling is wrong, crime is wrong.' He was overcome with exhaustion, frustration and sadness. He was devastated that he'd let his life drift this far down the wrong track. While Bill prepared to set off for the cave, Ned continued to stare into the flames, his mind working on a plan.

The children started the descent down the steep incline towards the cave. Hayley led the way, treading carefully, holding hands with Adam who was holding hands with Sophie. Ben was scrambling down the rocks as sure-footed as a mountain goat. Lara buzzed around them barking wildly. She wasn't sure which was worse, the act of climbing down a dangerous path or actually reaching the bottom where the smugglers could be waiting.

Hayley was getting impatient with the barking. 'Lara, will you please be quiet. We're trying to tread carefully and it's really difficult to do with you yapping in my ear. What on earth is wrong with you?'

'She's never been like this before,' said Ben apologetically. 'I think she senses there's something wrong; we just haven't worked out what.'

It was at that moment that Adam twigged. All of a sudden it came to him in a blinding flash of inspiration.

' "Juggler" with an "SM" is "smuggler",' he shouted. 'It's not "jugglers", it's "smugglers".' He beamed at his brilliance and then his face sank as he realized what he'd said.

Lara immediately stopped barking, stood

on her hindlegs and applauded the young man. Next she bowed repeatedly to him like a football fan worshipping a favourite player. The children stopped in their tracks.

'Smugglers?' echoed Hayley. 'Don't be daft.'

'Smugglers,' laughed Sophie. 'What, treasure and coins and things? I don't think so.'

Adam had already scrambled halfway back up the cliff. 'We certainly don't want to be going down there if there are smugglers,' he shouted. 'That's far too risky.'

Lara remained upright, continuing to nod vigorously. She pointed down the path and put her paw to her mouth, signalling shush. *I've seen them and heard them. This is most definitely real.*

Hayley continued to laugh it off. 'Stop being so pathetic,' she shouted back at

Adam. 'As if. This is so ridiculous. You'll be telling us there are pirates down there next.'

Sophie's eyes grew big and Adam the not-so-brave scrambled higher still. Smugglers? Pirates? This sounded very dangerous indeed.

Lara glanced anxiously over her shoulder and saw two figures in the distance. *Bill and Ned*, she panicked. *The dog smugglers are coming. They're really coming. There's no time to lose*. Lara stood on her hindlegs and pointed into the distance. *The baddies are on their way. We have no choice but to hide in the cave. Please understand*. Lara raised her hackles and produced a sinister growl in her throat. The mood immediately changed and Lara ushered the worried-looking children across the rocks and into the cave. Adam tried to escape but she expertly rounded him up, like she'd seen sheepdogs do on the TV. *In you go*, she urged. *Now scatter and hide*, she signalled, waving her paws in all directions. *Baddies are coming. And shush*. The children disappeared deep into the cave and took positions behind rocks, waiting for Lara's next instruction.

A minute later they heard men's voices echoing in the cave. 'Shine the torch, idiot, these rocks are slippery.'

The children shrank back into the darkness. They could hear dog barks echoing in the distance. Adam's teeth were chattering and Lara was afraid that the baddies would hear him. The smugglers lumbered closer. Ned stopped next to Adam's hiding place and struck a match, lighting the cave with an eerie glow. Adam held his breath and wedged his tongue between his teeth to shut them up. He wished he'd chosen a better hiding place, where his head didn't stick out. He could see the orangey glow of a cigarette coming his way and felt sure he was about to be discovered.

Lara was cringing. She felt Adam's fear, so she had no choice but to distract the smugglers. *Here goes*, she thought, leaping out of her hiding place with a bark. *Here I am, guys. Over here. Shine your torch this way.* A powerful light immediately picked Lara out, her eyes shining in the blackness. *Peekaboo. Come and get me,* she waved.

'One of the mutts has escaped and it's

waving at us,' bellowed Bill, surprise rising in his voice. 'Catch it, Ned.'

Ned's huge frame grabbed at Lara but she nipped through his legs and was away, towards the sunlight. Ned was after her, lumbering clumsily across the rocks. Lara heard a yell as he slipped and came crashing down in the darkness, slamming his knee against a rock. The children heard him curse.

'M . . . missed it,' he stammered.

'Idiot,' shouted Bill. 'You must have left one of the cages open. I only saw one mutt, so let it go. We'll never catch it, anyhow. We've still got dozens of the creatures to smuggle to the lorry. Let's get a move on.'

Adam dared to open his eyes. He watched as the two men clambered towards the back of the cave, their torches lighting up dozens of cages, the yapping getting louder as they approached.

Lara beckoned the children out of the cave. Carefully they slunk their way towards the light and, once in the open air, ran for their lives. They scrambled up the path, jumped into the tent and zipped it up, gasping for breath.

'Boy, that was close,' panted Hayley.

'They were real smugglers,' gasped Adam. 'I told you this was dangerous. I'm phoning Mum and the police.' He fumbled in his rucksack and pulled out his mobile. The others watched as he dialled frantically. His face dropped, theirs mirroring his despair. 'No signal,' he whispered. 'I told you we shouldn't have come into this wilderness.' He turned angrily on Lara. 'I can't believe you could bring us somewhere so remote and so dangerous.'

All eyes fell on the dog. Lara tried to stay calm. She reached for her two special spy-dog collars and clipped them round her neck. *OK, so this holiday hasn't quite gone according to plan. But I'll take charge and do what's best. Remember your training, Lara. I must do what's safest for the children.* She figured that the smugglers would be a while transferring the dogs back to the farmhouse. *There may be a phone there, or some transport that we can use. If we go now, we can beat the men to their hideout. Maybe even set a trap.*

11. Mad Max

Lara bounded off across the mainland in the direction of the abandoned farm. *Follow me, kids,* she urged. There were rabbits on the way but she hardly noticed. She galloped ahead of the children, forgetting about Max. Suddenly, from out of nowhere, he jumped on her, using his size and power to good advantage. Lara was knocked to the ground.

'Hello, dog,' he growled. 'We meet again.'

Lara recovered her poise and growled back, 'Look, mutt, whoever you are, my owners are in trouble and I need to find out what's going on around here. Your owners have stolen a lot of dogs. This is very serious, so let me through.'

'Serious, is it?' growled Max. 'I don't think so. But what I'm about to do to you is

102

serious. Maxy boy is going to tear you to shreds. We don't like strangers here. Bye bye, poochie dog.' He leapt on to Lara again, his claws tearing into her shoulder, knocking her off balance once more. The wound started to sting and Lara glanced at the blood seeping from the deep scratch marks.

She growled again and raised her hackles. She could probably take this dog out with judo or karate, but she thought she'd try something a bit cleverer. *Let's play the dumb defenceless animal and pander to his aggression.* Lara went all doe-eyed. She put on her best girlie voice and woofed, 'Please, Mr Max, please don't hurt me because I'm no match for your cleverness and speed.'

Max sat upright and stretched his neck with pride. Perhaps she was right. He considered himself to be rather clever and supremely fast. 'You are one of those really fast Dobermanns, aren't you?' said Lara, egging him on. 'I bet you catch loads of sheep. Mind you, even I can catch sheep – they're really slow, aren't they?' she giggled.

Max smiled. Yes, they were, although he'd never actually caught one.

'I bet you can catch rabbits too, can't you?' barked Lara. 'I mean, a dog of your speed and agility. I bet you catch a lot.'

Max frowned. Actually, he was a bit too slow and clumsy to catch rabbits, but he did like chasing them. One day he'd catch one for sure, and tear it limb from limb.

Lara looked sad. 'I can only catch rabbits when I wear my special speed-boost collar. This one,' she said pointing to her blue collar. 'My owners designed it especially for me. It makes me run extra fast so I can catch rabbits. Of course,' she teased, 'they said it's mine and no other dog must ever wear it.' As she hoped, Max couldn't resist. Sure, he would tear this dog limb from limb, but not until he'd had a go with that special collar. It sounded great – speed boost – just what he needed. Maybe he could catch a rabbit. Max couldn't believe his luck. Lara couldn't believe his stupidity.

'Give it here,' he woofed. 'Give me that collar and I'll let you go,' he lied.

Lara played the lady in distress, overacting terribly, beginning to have fun. 'Oh no, no. I couldn't. It's mine and I mustn't let you have it. You would be too fast for your own good.'

Max's excitement was too much to bear. He struggled out of his own metal-studded collar and threw it to the ground. Lara carefully removed her blue collar and secured it round Max's thick neck. She pretended to fumble with the buckle but was really clicking the combination to ARGH451EEK. There was a small beep and the electrical device was armed: *120 seconds and counting.* 'Please don't run off with my collar,' she pleaded, eyelashes fluttering. Her heart was pounding and her eyes frantically searching for somewhere to hide. She didn't mind his eyes lighting up but she didn't want shocking herself. She was calmly counting in her head.

One hundred seconds. 'It's too tight,' grunted the Dobermann. 'Loosen it a notch.'

Lara did as she was told, paws fumbling with excitement.

Eighty seconds left. Max stood there admiring himself.

Run away and chase a rabbit, for heaven's sake, thought Lara. *Stop posing and run. You're about to go buzz and I don't want to be near.*

Fifty seconds to go. Lara was starting to panic. Max was still here, standing next to her. *What happens if that collar starts shooting electric shocks or, even worse, he wants to swap back again?* She tried to stay calm.

'Do you feel any faster?' she asked. 'I mean, I can catch rabbits when I'm wearing it. Once I start running I go like the clappers.'

Max trotted around Lara eyeing her up. *Thirty seconds left.* 'Yes, I feel quite fast,' he admitted. 'I do feel kind of awesome.' He was vain but not as stupid as she thought. He'd worked out that if he ran off in one direction she might run off in the other.

'Well, for goodness' sake show me how fast you can go. Just pick a direction and run. Go on, run,' she urged, the panic rising in her bark. She wished she'd just duffed him up like she knew she could. Her clever plan wasn't looking so smart any more.

Suddenly he said, 'OK, poochie. Watch my electric pace.' She felt a surge of relief. He decided that if he was wearing a speed-boost collar he could go and catch a rabbit, then come and catch this girl dog afterwards. Max took a deep breath and shot off towards the coast, lolloping along like the slow, clumsy mutt he always had been. The fact was he'd probably not catch a tortoise never mind a rabbit, but he thought he was fast and that was making him happy. He bounded through the heather barking with glee. 'Look out, rabbits, here comes the new electrifying Maxy.'

Lara had darted behind a granite rock, peering round at Max as he bounded across the moors. In her head she was still counting: *5 . . . 4 . . . 3 . . . 2 . . . 1 . . .* Right on cue he sprang into the air, legs rigid, as the electric current surged through his body. He quickly recovered and started running again. He had only gone a few more metres before another surge took him by surprise, this one standing his fur on end and making him froth at the mouth. He shook wildly, dog slobber spraying everywhere. *This speed-boost collar isn't all it was cracked up to be.* He galloped back towards Lara, racked with electricity twice more.

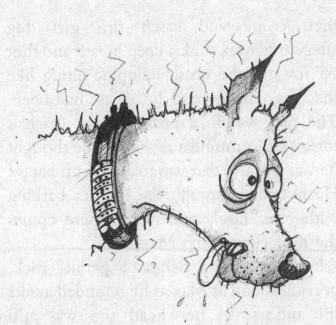

'Err, can you get this thing off me, mutt? It's making me feel strange,' he barked.

'Sorry, Maxy,' barked Lara. 'You keep the collar on until you've learned some manners.'

'Why, you horrible –' began Max, before being cut short by another bolt of electricity. He looked spiky like a toilet brush, but his shoulders slumped and his eyes drooped. The collar was working exactly as the professor said. The big dog was close to surrender.

Lara looked at the wound on her

shoulder. 'What about this, Max?' she barked. 'Why should I help you?'

Max hung his head. 'I'm sorry about that,' he whined. 'I was following orders, that's all. It was stupid of me. I promise never to do anything bad again.'

Lara felt a twinge of pity for the bloodthirsty dog. 'Tell you what, Maxy,' she barked, 'if you behave and do exactly what I say, I'll see what I can do about the speed-boost collar.'

Max was desperate. He knew he had no choice. His heavy head nodded, so Lara stepped forward and fumbled with the collar, disarming the device. 'There you go, big fellah,' she woofed. 'I've sorted it. But if you ever step out of line or forget your manners, I will switch it back on. Understand?' Max understood perfectly. 'I need your help with a couple of things, OK? If you help me out, I'll make sure the collar gets removed completely.'

Max's eyes lit up with hope rather than electricity. 'Just name it,' he pleaded. 'I'll do anything to get rid of this wretched speed-boost collar.'

Ben, Sophie, Adam and Hayley finally arrived, jogging wearily.

'The collar stays on, Maxy boy, until you've been useful to me. And that means taking care of my owners. Deal?'

Max looked at the ground. 'Deal,' he muttered.

Max led the way to a huge rock and the children collapsed in a heap, just as Lara spied Bill and Ned coming over the hill. They were pulling a trolley, loaded with cages. As they came closer Lara could hear furious yapping. *Think, Lara, think. This is going to need a spy-dog solution.* She watched as the men loaded the cages into the back of a lorry. Bill bolted the back door and rubbed his hands. 'That's it, then, mate.' He grinned. 'Wait until dark and off we go.'

12. Tall Stories

Lara watched as Ned lit another fire, intending to wile away an hour or two before driving to the meeting point. Bill went over the plan one last time. They had arranged to meet the buyer at midnight at the motorway services. They would hand over most of the dogs and collect their money from this man, a whopping £50,000.

'We then move to another town and start stealing dogs all over again. It's an act of criminal genius,' smiled Bill. 'Especially when we can get huge rewards for returning dogs to the owners we stole them from in the first place.' He laughed until his smoker's cough took over.

Lara shuddered as he cleared his throat and spat into the fire.

As usual, Bill explained and Ned listened. Bill conveniently left out the bit where he double-crosses his mate and runs off with all the cash. Ned was planning the bit where he double-crosses Bill and lets the dogs go free. They exchanged crocodile smiles, each scheming against the other.

Lara listened carefully. She now knew their whole plan; she just needed one of her own. She was just about to sprint across to the children when she saw someone stumbling through the bracken, heading for the old farmhouse. As he came closer she could see he was cold and bedraggled. The poor man was soaked to the skin. He was pale and drawn and looked in need of some warmth. He was carrying a camera, an expensive one by the look of it, the sort that newspaper photographers use. Lara remained hidden while the man staggered closer. *Most curious indeed.*

Dusk was setting in and the glow of the fire must have looked appealing to the drenched photographer. He staggered into the rickety farmhouse and Lara heard him talking to Bill and Ned.

'Hello, guys. I'm looking for some shelter from the rain. Do you mind if I come in and warm myself a bit?' he asked through chattering teeth.

Lara jumped up to the paneless window and peeped into the room. She saw the startled expressions on Bill and Ted's faces. The photographer noticed it too.

'Sorry,' he exclaimed. 'Didn't mean to make you jump or disturb you, but I'm freezing to death. I've spent two nights sleeping rough.' Nothing seemed to register on the other faces. 'Starving hungry, wet through,' he explained.

Ned said nothing. What was the point? He'd just get stuck on the first syllable and then Bill would ridicule him like he always did. Then this visitor would think he was stupid. *Better to think you're quiet than stupid*, thought Ned.

Bill grunted. 'Come in for a minute, seeing as you already have.'

The photographer shifted towards the fire, holding his hands out to embrace the warmth.

'What are you doing here, anyway?'

113

grunted Bill. 'On the run or sommat?'

The photographer wasn't stupid. Here were two men sitting in an old farmhouse in the middle of nowhere, surrounded by rubbish. Neither man looked like he had washed in a week and both smelt terrible. He wasn't going to impress them with niceties. 'I'm looking for a dog,' he said, glancing at the empty cages stacked around the room. 'Don't suppose you've seen mine around?'

Bill eyed him suspiciously. 'A dog?' he repeated, looking at his partner. 'We've got loads of dogs, ain't we, Ned? If you've got the cash we've got the mutt for you. We are sort of "dog collectors", see. What sort is it that you're after?'

The reporter studied the cages. 'It's a highly trained super dog actually. It can do loads of special tricks and has got a keen sense of smell and, boy, is it fast.'

Bill looked up, interested, his piggy eyes glinting in the firelight. 'Sounds like my Max,' he said proudly. 'We've not seen him for a while. Has he been chasing you?' he asked, eyes shining with pride at the thought of Max causing trouble.

'It's me doing the chasing,' explained the photographer. 'The dog I'm tracking is a female. Lara, she's called. Black and white. Ugly mutt if you ask me, one ear up and one ear down.'

Lara nearly fell off the window sill with surprise. She pricked up her ears and listened as hard as she could. *He's looking for me? This is getting interesting. And did he call me ugly?*

'This dog I'm after is going to make me loads of money. And I mean loads,' purred the photographer, rubbing his hands together with greed.

Bill mirrored his body language. Those three special little words 'loads of money' always made his heart flutter. 'How's that, then?' he asked, trying to sound casual.

'Like I say, she's a special mutt, bred by the Secret Service. She's trying to keep her identity secret but I've got a whole load of photos that show what she can really do. I've been following her and some kids for the last couple of days and you won't believe the shots I've got in here,' he said, patting his camera. 'Truly awesome stuff of the dog juggling, playing pool and even riding a bike. Imagine what they're worth to the tabloids.'

Bill snorted. 'A dog riding a bike? Yeah, right, mate.'

'And she surfs too,' piped up the photographer. 'She can catch a good wave.'

Lara smiled. *He's right. But how does he know?*

The photographer reached into his coat pocket and pulled out a crumpled photo. 'Take a look,' he said passing it to Bill

Bill took it and his smile evaporated, his piggy eyes widening. It was a picture of a black and white dog riding a bike, ears flapping in the wind. 'Incredible. We saw this mutt in the cave. Blasted thing waved at us, didn't it, Ned?' He gave the photo to Ned, whose long face stretched even further into a look of silent surprise. 'How much are your pictures worth?' enthused Bill, this time failing to conceal his excitement.

'Dunno precisely,' replied the photographer. 'Depends how the rest of them turn out, I suppose. I can either sell them to the government, tell them, "Give me a million quid or I go public", or flog them to the papers. Might even get into a bidding war between the tabloids.'

Bill had stopped listening at the point where the photographer had said 'a million quid'. This really was loads of money and he felt a dastardly plan coming on. His mind was whirring. He needed to get his hands on the camera and any films this man had in his pocket. He would have let Max loose on him but the dog seemed to have disappeared. He decided to try and outdo the photographer's story. 'Me and Ned here are going to make stacks of money too. Easy money. Tonight. Aren't we, Ned?'

Now it was the photographer's turn to pin back his ears and listen. 'Tonight?' he echoed. Greed was his number-one quality and he loved the idea of instant cash.

'Yes, tonight. We've got hundreds of pedigree mutts loaded into that lorry parked outside. All we have to do is drop them off at the motorway services at midnight tonight and we get £100,000,' he exaggerated. 'Some are rare breeds that fetch thousands in rewards from their grateful owners. Criminal geniuses we are.'

The photographer whistled softly. 'A hundred thousand. That's a lot of dosh.'

'B . . . b . . . but that's n . . . n . . . n . . .' stammered Ned.

'But that's nice, he's trying to say,' soothed Bill, 'And the cash'll be in our pockets by midnight.'

Ned spat into the fire and stormed out into the rain. He was trying to say, 'But that's not right, Bill. Stealing dogs is a crime. Think of how many people we've upset. I'm having none of it.' How come he could say it in his head but not transfer it to his tongue? Life was so unfair.

Ned stood in the doorway and fought with his emotions. He was a grown man, he mustn't cry. But life was dreadful. He wanted to get out of the trouble he'd got himself into and he didn't know how, so the tears came – in silent floods.

Lara jumped down from the window sill and studied Ned. *What a terribly sad man he must be,* she thought. *If he doesn't want to be part of this, maybe he'll help me. What have I got to lose?* Lara approached the big man, appearing out of the semi-darkness. He saw her through his tears, a blurred vision of black and white, one ear up and one down. He wiped a dirty sleeve across his face smearing his tears and runny nose across his cheek.

'D . . . D . . . D . . .' he pointed at her. Then he pointed inside, remembering the picture he'd just seen.

Yes, I'm the bike-riding dog that the photographer is going to destroy, thought Lara. *He's going to ruin my life and make me into some sort of freak show. And you are the man that Bill's going to destroy. We've got a lot in common. We can both understand but can't speak for a start!* Lara stood on her hindlegs and put her paw across her mouth, signifying 'shush'. Ned looked behind him, expecting Bill to appear at any minute. Lara beckoned to him to come outside and hesitantly he trudged out into the drizzle. Lara remained on her hindlegs, walked up to him and licked him on the cheek to signal that she wanted his friendship. *Yuk, tears and snot,* she thought, doing a doggie grimace. The big man didn't notice: he'd got a friend; he'd had very few of those.

Lara opened his coat and he allowed her to take out his mobile. She switched it on and was relieved to see it was picking up a weak signal. She typed 999, holding it out to Ned so he could speak to the police, offering him the opportunity to right his wrong. *Go on, tell the police what's going on and put a stop to this right now.* Ned put the phone to his ear and listened. It rang and then someone answered. 'Hello, which emergency service would you like?'

'P . . . P . . .' began Ned. He stopped and took a deep breath. *Come on, man, get a grip,* he told himself. *You can say it in your head. Now let your mouth take charge. This is very important. One, two, three . . . go.* 'P . . . P . . . P . . .' *Doh.* He so badly wanted to say, 'Police, please. I'd like to report a dog-smuggling gang and a baddy photographer', but he couldn't get past the first letter.

For heaven's sake, thought Lara, getting impatient. *OK, we'll try something different.* She took the mobile and started to type a text message, which is very difficult with paws instead of hands. Still, she managed, and clicked 'OK' to send it on its way. The message read:

dear prof danger need hlp mway servis
midnite bring polis gm451

Then she took off her collar and pressed the secret button to release the catch. Two tiny pills fell into her paw and she solemnly handed them to Ned. *Now's your chance, big fellah,* she thought. She pointed to an empty beer can from the floor and pretended to drop the pills into it. Then she rolled on the floor squirming in pretend agony. Next she jumped to her feet and pointed inside the farmhouse. *Go and put these pills into their drinks,* she urged. *Please understand. Please be on my side.*

Ned understood perfectly. This super sophisticated dog was his way out and he intended to take it. He slipped the pills into his pocket, turned on his heel and went back inside.

Mum had tried to ring the children a dozen times but they hadn't answered, so she was relieved when the mobile eventually rang. 'That'll be them, at last,' she said, fumbling in her handbag.

'Hello,' Dad heard her say. 'Oh, Professor Cortex, it's you,' she continued, sounding surprised. 'What do you mean, do I know where the children and Lara are?' she said, her voice registering panic. 'They're camping, somewhere on the coast . . . aren't they?' After a few seconds, Mum finished on the phone, her face white.

'What is it?' asked Dad.

'Lara's sent a text message to the professor which says they're in danger. The professor's sending a car for us any minute now.'

13. On the Move

Mum, Dad and Ollie were dropped off in a supermarket car park, in the dead of night. The driver pointed in the direction of a delivery van. 'That's your meeting point,' he explained. 'Your coded reply is, "Yes, please, delivered straight to my door."'

The three of them approached the van, feeling a bit silly. Dad knocked gingerly and the back door opened slightly, bright light flooding out of the crack. A silhouetted figure stood in the gap. 'Groceries, sir?'

Dad looked around at the others before clearing his throat. 'Err, yes, please. Delivered straight to my door?'

The door opened fully and the three of them stepped into the Secret Service vehicle.

★

Lara beckoned the children out from behind the rock.

Adam wouldn't move. 'Too dangerous,' he said. 'You are supposed to be a super dog, so it's up to you to do something super. I'm staying put.'

The other three children helped Lara with her half of the plan. Hayley carefully undid the bolt and the three gently lowered the lorry's tailgate. Lara barked a quiet instruction to the caged dogs.

'Ladies and gents,' she said, 'we are here to rescue you and return you to your owners. You just need to trust us and be absolutely silent.'

The children undid the cages and one by one the dogs slunk

out of the lorry and joined Adam behind the rock.

Now for part two of my plan, thought Lara. She instructed Max, Princess Teensie and two other dogs to round up some sheep. 'As many as you can, and as quietly as you can,' she urged. 'I want them herded into the back of the lorry, and we haven't got much time.' The dogs went about their business, no questions asked. This strange mutt had rescued them from their cages and said she would return them home, so they would do as she said.

A dozen sheep were herded into the back of the lorry. *Now close the tailgate,* she urged. Ben, Hayley and Sophie were struggling to lift it when Lara heard one of the smugglers rattling the farmhouse door. Bill lumbered out into the fresh air and Lara panicked. She stuffed Max and the girls into the back of the lorry and heaved the tailgate into place. Lara and Ben sneaked under the lorry, controlling their breathing. Bill stood a few metres away, rolling his cigarette. Lara watched his feet as he walked to the back of the lorry, and she heard him padlock the tailgate. 'Just to make sure you doggies don't escape,' he grinned, before returning indoors.

Lara grimaced. *Whoops. That wasn't supposed to happen. I've rescued the dogs but trapped the kids. But at least the professor can track the lorry through Max's collar. Don't worry, girls*, she thought, *I've not given up on you yet.*

'Let us out,' murmured Hayley, her fists pummelling the canvas sides.

'I can't,' hissed Ben. 'The bloke has padlocked the door. Be quiet or they'll hear you. You'll just have to stay in there until Lara works out a rescue plan.'

Mmm, could be a tricky one. Lara sneaked back to the window sill, trying not to pant, keen to see if Ned would administer the pills.

The two talkers were in full flow, both exaggerating how much money they were going to make.

'I once sold some pictures of a soap star on a beach holiday for half a million quid,' boasted the press man. 'And some pics of a pop star for a hundred thousand pounds.'

'That's now't,' said Bill. 'I once did a bank job that netted nearly a million,' he lied. It was true that he'd once done a bank job but all it had netted him was six years in prison.

Ned tried to join in. 'Anyone want a d . . . d . . . d,' he began, stuttering like a cold car engine.

'A "d . . . d . . . d",' mocked Bill. 'What's a "d . . . d . . . d", may I ask? A d . . . d . . . donkey? A d . . . d . . . daffodil? Idiot. If you can't spit it out, then don't bother. Just keep your trap shut.' Bill loved showing off and Ned was easy to bully.

But Ned was feeling calm. His decision was now made. Instead of going along with the smuggling plot he was going to work with the spy dog to bring this whole criminal network down. He told himself to relax and just go along with these fools. 'D . . . d . . . drink,' he blurted, pointing to the cans in the corner of the room.

'Oh, a drink! Not as stupid as you look, eh, mate?' mocked Bill. 'Yes, crack some open and we can celebrate our biggest pay day ever.'

Bill and his new friend continued their ridiculous conversation while Ned pulled three cans from the pack. His heart was pounding. Could he get the pills in without the guys noticing? Lara watched, hardly daring to breathe as Ned reached into his pocket and fingered the pills. His eyes darted around the room, catching Lara's gaze from the window. She nodded in encouragement and Ned quickly looked away.

'Where's that drink, idiot?' called Bill. 'Are you slow as well as stupid?'

Ned was too angry to reply. His hands were shaking uncontrollably as he tugged at the first ring pull, nearly dropping the can on the floor. Bill and his friend hardly noticed, engrossed in their conversation. Lara was willing him on. *Go, Ned, go. Drop a pill into the can and hand it to one of them.*

Ned held it in his shaking left hand and felt in his right pocket, pulling out a pill and holding it in his clumsy fingers. He turned his back to the pair and slipped the green pill into the first can. What a relief, now all he had to do was make one of them drink it.

Ned walked towards the photographer and offered him the can.

'Cheers, mate,' said the press man gratefully, taking a massive swig. He wiped his sleeve across his mouth and belched.

Ned shuffled back to the corner and opened the second can, this one exploding with a massive hiss, froth spraying up the wall. Once again he reached into his pocked, fumbling for the other pill. He pulled it out but the tiny tablet escaped from his awkward hands, dropping on to the dirt floor. Watching from the window, Lara gasped in frustration. She could hardly look.

'Is that drink coming or what?' bellowed Bill. 'I'm g . . . g . . . gasping,' he mocked, howling with laughter at his cruel joke.

Ned managed a watery smile but didn't bother trying to answer. His speech may let him down but his mind had never been clearer. He bent down and pretended to pull another can from the pack. The pink pill was tiny but he managed to grip it between his thumb and forefinger, dropping it into Bill's drink before offering it to him.

'And one for yourself, me old mate,' urged Bill. 'We don't want to drink on our own.'

Pulling the third tab was the last thing Ned could remember. Lara watched in silent agony as Bill tiptoed across the room, metal bar in hand, and thudded the weapon across the big man's shoulders. Ned fell to his knees, groggy and dazed. The big man was powerless as Bill sat on him and began looping a rope round his wrists and ankles. Within minutes he was expertly trussed up, Bill stuffing one of his dirty socks into Ned's mouth for good measure.

'That should do the trick,' smirked Bill, observing his handiwork. Ned wriggled but there was no chance of escape. 'Three's a crowd, mate,' laughed Bill. 'I was getting the vibes that you wasn't too keen on this mutt-smuggling caper, anyway, so this is your way out.'

'Blimey, mate, that was a bit harsh,' said

the newspaper man, scared he might be next. 'I didn't want you to hurt him, just get him out of the picture, so we can share the cash.'

'And that's exactly what I have done,' snarled Bill. The first part of his plan had worked, now there was just the photographer to dispose of. 'Just finish your drink and let's be on our way,' he ordered. 'No time to waste.'

Both men drank up, draining every last drop. Bill let out a raucous burp and crumpled his can. The photographer followed suit and both men stumbled out of the farmhouse into the rain. Bill went round to the back of the lorry to double check the tailgate was securely padlocked. Then both men jumped into the cab and Bill started the engine. He spent a minute getting used to the buttons and switches before the lorry pulled away, slowly heading down the farm track towards the road. Lara beckoned Adam and Ben to follow, sixty silent dogs wagging close behind. Luckily the potholes kept the speed at a snail's pace.

The lorry stopped up ahead. Lara and the boys approached slowly, half crouched. As Lara edged nearer she heard a terrible groaning noise coming from the lorry. Bill leapt from the cab and rushed into the bracken, before an explosion erupted from his bottom.

Ahh, he must have had the pink pill, thought Lara. *Severe tummy trouble. The professor said it was almost instantaneous!*

Bill also had another problem. He needed a change of trousers. Lara watched as a half-naked Bill jumped back into the cab and shouted to his partner in crime, 'I've had a bit of an accident, mate. Must be nerves or something.'

There was no answer. The photographer was slumped in his seat, snoring like a baby.

Ah, the green pill, thought Lara.

Bill shook his new friend but there was no response. He slapped the photographer across the face. There was still no response, so he slapped him again. He lifted the photographer's eyelids and there was just white underneath. 'Blimey, mate, two days' sleeping rough has really worn you out. You must be exhausted to sleep this deep.' Bill spent the next five minutes removing the photographer's trousers and putting them on himself, before pulling the sleeping body from the cab and dumping it in the bracken. 'And I'll just look after these for you,' he said, removing the camera from round the photographer's neck and the reels of film from his coat pocket. Bill then jumped back into the cab and crunched the lorry into gear.

Lara approached the photographer and gave him a quick check. He was all right, just sound asleep, cheeks blowing in and out like bellows. She chased after the lorry, following at a discreet distance. A few hundred metres down the track the lorry stopped again, Bill jumping out and running into the trees once more. This time there were serious cries of pain like Lara had never heard before.

While Bill sorted himself out, she and the boys ran on ahead. Lara had half a plan. All she needed was a big slice of luck.

14. Hot Pursuit

Lara needed to find transport of her own, because when Bill reached the tarmac road the lorry would just accelerate away and she'd never keep up. The dirt track broadened out into a proper road through a village. It was late at night and not a soul was about. Lara considered her options – left was open road, right was a church, a garage and a few houses. A blue motorway sign pointed right, so she guessed this would be the way Bill would go. The boys were exhausted. Lara reckoned they had about ten minutes before the lorry arrived.

They ventured into the village. Lara had a good sniff around before she had the dose of good luck she was after. She spied a house with a motorbike parked in the drive, a big Harley-Davidson like she'd seen in the movies. She'd always wanted to ride one and now she just needed to work out how to get the keys. She ran around the back of the house, assuming no lights meant everyone was asleep. She looked at the church clock: 11.20. *Just forty minutes until Bill's meeting with the gang ringleader. I have to make this plan work first time.* She tried the back door but it was locked. An open window on the first floor gave her an idea. She went next door to where she'd seen a ladder leaning up against the house and struggled back with it. The boys watched as she put it up to the first-floor window. *I hope nobody sees me*, she thought as she climbed carefully up the rungs. *I've heard of cat burglars, but I think the newspapers would have a field day with a dog burglar!*

Bill's stomach was swollen with wind and the pain was terrible. It came in waves and when his guts signalled go, it really was time to go. He clenched his bottom, but he couldn't hold the pressure as another

eruption of wind nearly raised him off the driving seat. He wound down the window, wafting his hand across his face to hasten the clearing of the smell. His stomach churned and he felt the pressure building again. But he had to continue the journey. If he missed the midnight meeting he would lose the £50,000 payment, so he grimaced in pain and floored the accelerator. Hayley, Sophie and the sheep were thrown around in the back of the lorry.

Bill pulled on to the main road and

headed towards the motorway, roaring through the village. He kept seeing dogs everywhere. 'Must be imagining things,' he murmured. He was ill. His stomach was making gurgling noises like a chemistry laboratory. Sweat rolled down his cheeks and his vision was blurred. Through the open window he saw a black and white dog climbing up a ladder. He took his eyes off the road and focused his gaze. *Dogs can't climb ladders, can they?* He wasn't sure of anything any more, perhaps he was hallucinating. He looked again and the dog was gone. He emitted another massive blast of wind. *Must be seeing things,* he thought as he shifted into top gear and coaxed maximum speed from the lorry.

Mum, Dad and Ollie stepped into the Secret Service van. The professor sat at a bank of keyboards and TV screens. There were more buttons than Ollie had ever seen and he put his hands deep into his pockets to resist the temptation.

'What on earth's going on?' demanded Mum. 'Why have you called us here and where are the children? And what do you mean by danger?'

The professor looked up from his computers. 'Received this message from agent GM451 at twenty-two seventeen,' he said, beaming the text message on to a screen. 'And then at twenty-three zero three we started to track movement, through GM451's collar.' Another screen showed a map, with a tiny blue dot beeping along one of the roads. 'Keeps stopping, but most definitely on the move.' Dad thought the professor looked slightly nervous. 'Looks like your children might have been camping near the site of a dog-smuggling ring that we've been watching for some time.'

Mum gulped. 'Are they dangerous?'

The professor mopped his brow. He tapped his keyboard and Bill's piggy face appeared on one of the screens. 'William Bernhard Blyth, aka 'Pit Bull'. A criminal record as long as both your arms. I wouldn't want your children to bump into him on a dark night.'

'But this is a dark night ... and they have,' noted Dad. 'So where are they now?'

All eyes were drawn to the blue dot. 'Heading north towards the motorway,' the professor said, pointing. 'Let's go and meet them.'

15. Motorcycle Mutt

Lara heard the lorry roar by as she dropped through the window. She padded silently across the landing and down the stairs. *No time to waste. To stand any chance of rescuing the girls we have to catch the lorry before it reaches the motorway.* All was dark and quiet. There was a big bunch of keys conveniently hanging from a hook in the kitchen. *These must be the ones,* she told herself as she clasped them between her paws. The clinking noise woke the family cat, curled up in the comfort of a kitchen chair. He looked faintly surprised at the presence of a dog in the house. He half-opened his eyes and mewed at Lara, which, translated, meant: 'It's the middle of the night. And what on earth are you doing in my house, anyway?'

Lara could understand Cat but couldn't speak it. Maybe this cat could understand Dog, so she quietly woofed, 'Just borrowing the keys for the motorbike, OK, puss? I've got to get to the motorway services. Please apologize to the owner.' The cat blinked a couple of times before curling back into a ball and falling fast asleep. *Typical feline,* thought Lara. *They just can't be bothered. I suppose that's why the professor's given up trying to develop a spy cat.*

Lara picked up the helmet lying on the kitchen table and fitted it over her head, carefully fastening the strap under her chin. Then she took the leather jacket from the hook behind the door and struggled into it. *No point in taking unnecessary risks,* she thought. She picked up some goggles and two more helmets before expertly opening the front door and letting herself out on to the drive.

Ben and Adam were waiting beside the highly polished Harley which gleamed in the moonlight. Lara threw each a helmet. *Here you go, guys. You'll be needing these.* Lara the biker dog mounted the Harley and, taking the key in her mouth, managed to get it into

the ignition. She pressed the push-button starter and the motorbike roared into life, its engine sounding gruff and throaty. *How cool is this?* she smiled as she used both her paws to rev the machine. She beckoned to the disbelieving boys. *Come on, guys, I'm going to need help to drive this thing. It's the only way to rescue Sophie and Hayley.*

Ben climbed straight aboard, revving the motorbike, encouraging its throaty roar.

Adam took some convincing. 'You cannot be serious? Of all the dangerous things to do . . .'

Ben and Lara rolled out of the drive on to the road, revving as if to leave Adam behind. The family pet fixed Adam with an icy stare. *We're deadly serious. The girls are in grave danger and we are their only chance.*

Adam quickly considered his options and decided the bike ride was less risky than being left alone in a strange village, at night. 'Wait for me,' he bellowed, as he sprinted towards them, squeezing in between Ben and Lara.

Ben worked the throttle and Lara the gears as they wheelspun the Harley on to the open road, destroying the calm of the night.

Lara calculated that the lorry had about a ten-minute head start, so they would need to shift a bit. Ben opened the throttle and the powerful machine wheelied, nearly throwing Lara off the back. Between them, they eventually mastered the controls and powered the machine down the empty road in hot pursuit of the lorry.

Alf was a regular at the Red Lion. He was always the last to leave and tonight was no exception. He was staggering home when the motorbike growled by. Lara, trying to play it cool, raised a paw and saluted him.

The old soldier saluted back. Then he stopped and thought for a second before turning and watching Lara speed off into the distance, tail blowing in the slipstream. There was no mistaking that it was a motorcycling dog.

Even with a helmet on it was as plain as the nose on his face. On the back of the jacket he could see the silver studs spelling out the words, 'Dogs of War'. *Three on a bike? . . . A motorcycling dog?* he thought. *Nahhh.* He shook his head and vowed to give up drinking.

16. A Daring Rescue

The trio roared through the night, the motorbike eating up the road. Ben spotted the lorry in the distance. 'There it is, up ahead,' he shouted above the noise of the Harley.

I see it, acknowledged Lara, *but I'm not quite sure what we're going to do when we catch up.*

The lumbering lorry soon came into range and the biker-three cruised behind. Ben, sitting at the front, was proving to be an expert with steering and acceleration. Lara, at the back, was superb at gear changes. Adam, the sandwich filling, still couldn't quite believe what was happening. He was gripping Ben so tightly that it was affecting his circulation.

Three miles to the motorway, Lara noticed from a sign. *I think this is time for action.* She tightened her helmet strap and pulled the goggles over her eyes. *This could get a bit hairy.*

Lara waved to Ben to move alongside the lorry.

'Not a good idea,' shouted Adam, who was so close to the vehicle that he could hear the tyres humming on the tarmac.

Ben did as he was told and expertly steered in parallel to the lorry.

Closer, please, pointed his pet. *If this is going to work we have to be almost touching.*

Ben inched towards the lorry so the vehicles were just an arm's width apart. The motorbike was now on the wrong side of the road and Ben could see headlights coming. Adam let go of his iron grip round Ben's waist and pointed ahead. 'A car, there's a car coming,' he panicked, stating the obvious.

Hold your nerve, Ben, thought Lara. *A bit closer . . . and just a tiny bit more . . . so we're nearly touching . . .*

Ben couldn't stay alongside any longer.

The oncoming car flashed its headlights and sounded its horn as it sped by. Bill swerved the lorry and the bike had no choice but to pull away and follow behind.

'That was close,' Ben shouted. 'Do you want to try again?'

But Lara had gone, springing like a cat rather than a dog, clinging to the side of the lorry with her claws and teeth. *Hold tight, Lara. Grip with those jaws.*

The boys stayed in the lorry's slipstream and watched as their pet struggled to pull herself on to its roof. She lay flat for a few seconds, recovering her composure. The boys then saw her crouched on the roof, surveying the scene. Lara could see traffic lights a mile ahead. *No time to lose*, she thought. *If this plan is to work, I have to rescue the girls before we stop at the lights . . . if we stop at the lights.*

She scampered across the soft canvas top, looking for the best way in. There was a slight tear which she decided was her only chance. Lara summoned all her strength and took an almighty bite at the canvas, grabbing a piece of the material between her powerful jaws. Then, with all her might, she pulled. The material came away much more easily than she expected and she careered backwards. Ben and Adam gasped as they saw Lara teetering towards the edge of the roof, her back legs dangling over the side. She righted herself, delighted to have made a massive hole in the roof of the lorry. She peered in at the sheep. Looking up at her were two very surprised girls. No words were necessary. Hayley stood and then fell back as the lorry swerved around a corner. Lara disappeared from sight again, the boys once more holding their breath as her legs dangled in space, her claws scrabbling for a hold.

Woah, she thought. *Hold tight, girl.* Lara could see the traffic lights. They were on green and she wanted red. *Please change, please, please, please,* she willed.

She returned to the hole and lowered a paw for Hayley to grab. Lara didn't have the strength to pull, but Hayley was strong and she managed to heave herself on to the roof. Hayley lay flat and helped haul up Sophie, leaving the sheep and Max below.

They hung on as the lorry slowed at the lights.

A red light, thank goodness, thought Lara.

The lorry stopped and the pet lowered the girls safely to the tarmac. The lights changed and the lorry pulled away. *Here goes.* Lara jumped off the roof, caught a lamp post and slid, firefighter–style, to the ground. They watched as the lorry turned left on to the motorway. Hayley, Adam, Ben, Sophie and Lara embraced in a team hug, followed by a high five.

'What a rescue!' crowed Adam, delighted that he'd played a part.

'Truly brilliant, Lara,' said Hayley.

'I told you, she's a spy dog,' said Ben, puffing out his chest. 'She's one in a million.'

Lara sat proudly, wagging her tail. *It wasn't bad, was it,* she considered. *A bit of luck at the traffic lights, but otherwise an inspired team effort.*

'I wonder what Bill's going to think when he gets to the meeting point and finds he's got a load of sheep instead of dogs,' laughed Hayley.

I vote we go and find out, woofed Lara,

mounting the Harley once more.

'Brilliant,' beamed Adam. 'Can I do the power and steering this time?'

The others looked at him, bewildered.

'But isn't it a bit dangerous?' asked Ben

'Who cares,' said Adam, his eyes shining. 'This is the best adventure ever.'

The supermarket delivery van pulled on to the motorway. It picked up speed and Dad saw they were gaining on the blue dot. A few minutes later they were in the middle lane alongside a lorry, necks straining to see who was driving. It was the man off the TV screen, his piggy eyes fixed on the tarmac ahead. He looked uncomfortable, almost in pain, and he was sweating.

'There's your blue dot,' explained the professor, matter-of-factly. 'I suspect GM451 and the children are in the back.'

Mum was much less matter-of-fact. 'What on earth are they doing in the back of a lorry?' she squealed. 'We need to rescue them, right now.'

'Don't worry, Mum,' shouted Ollie. 'They're not in the back.' He pointed to a motorbike that was overtaking them in the fast lane. Adam, Hayley, Ben, Sophie and Lara sped by, clinging to each other for dear life. 'See, no need to worry,' smiled Ollie.

Mum wilted into a comfy chair, her eyes glazed over with shock. 'You're right,' she whispered. 'Why bother worrying.'

17. A Sheepish Grin

Adam and his passengers turned into the motorway services. The Secret Service van was next in and Lara was relieved when it pulled up alongside. The back door opened and Professor Cortex acknowledged her presence, seemingly unsurprised at her mode of transport or the fact that there were four children as passengers. Mum squealed with relief and ushered the children into the safety of the van. Lara loosened her helmet and let it fall to the ground.

Agent K opened the front door and invited Lara in. She declined. The lorry lumbered into the car park and Lara pointed to it, indicating the presence of baddies. The professor nodded and the back door closed.

Bill was in agony, his stomach bloated to three times its normal size. He parked the lorry at the darkest end of the car park and switched off the engine. Almost immediately a car pulled out of the shadows and stopped next to the lorry. Lara stalked over to listen, discarding the leather jacket as she went.

Bill jumped down from the cab. The man in the car got out and pulled a briefcase from the passenger seat and showed it to Bill. Lara strained to listen to their conversation.

'It's all there – £50,000, like we agreed,' said the mystery man. 'Now, show me the hounds. Remember, I'm paying for top quality.'

Bill had never seen so much money. He forgot his stomach pains for a moment and reached out to touch the crisp notes. He wanted to count them, smell them, taste them.

The man snapped the briefcase shut. 'The dogs first,' he reminded. 'Or no loot.'

Bill walked to the back of the lorry. 'Don't you trust me?' he asked. 'You give me the dosh and I'll drop 'em off in London, like we agreed.'

'I want to know they're safe,' explained the middleman. 'I don't want to be double-crossed.'

Bill sighed impatiently. He reached up to the lock and pulled down the tailgate. 'I can guarantee top quality,' he said impatiently. 'Stole them . . . myself . . .' he said, his voice trailing away as Max walked gingerly down the tailgate. 'Maxy, how on earth did you get in there?' He looked at the money man. 'Max is mine,' he said. 'He's not part of the bargain.' Bill marched up the tailgate to fetch some of the dogs. After a few seconds he came back out, face white as the sheep within. Boy, was he having a bad day.

'Where are they, then?' enquired the man with the briefcase.

'Erm, I c . . . c . . . can explain,' blurted Bill catching Ned's stutter. 'It's like this, see . . .' he began, not knowing where his sentence was going. He had personally locked the tailgate on sixty-three pedigree dogs. He had counted them in one by one.

Somehow they had turned into sheep and he was confused. Wind whistled from his bottom again. 'Scuse me,' he apologized, 'I'm ill you see. Terrible tummy trouble. If you give me some more time I can find your dogs.'

A lone sheep wandered down the tailgate. 'Baa?' it enquired. Several others followed their leader.

The man with the briefcase didn't understand what was going on but felt sure he was being double-crossed – he was paying for dogs not sheep. He pulled a pistol from his jacket pocket and pointed it at Bill.

Staring down the barrel of a gun made Bill's stutter worse and he began to feel dreadful for ridiculing Ned.

'Like I s . . . s . . . said, I can explain,' he lied. How could dogs turn into sheep? He couldn't explain it at all.

Lara wandered into sight, not scared of the gun. Bill looked at her, 'Shoo, mutt,' he said. 'Stay away from these sheep.' Then he looked again and gradually it dawned on him who she was. Black and white, one ear up and one down, bullet hole in one ear, ugly, rides a bike . . . 'Spy dog!' he exclaimed. 'I've been set up.' Bill grinned at Max. 'Let's sort her out, shall we? Go get her, Maxy,' he bellowed. 'Tear that blasted spy dog to pieces.'

Max sat still, looking down at his paws. Lara raised an eyebrow. *I dare you, Maxy*, she thought. *One step closer and I'll turn your collar on again.*

'Go on, Max. Kill,' yelled Bill. 'What's the matter with you? I'm ordering you to attack.'

Max stood up and shot a quick glance at his owner, then at Lara. It was no contest. He walked slowly back up the tailgate to be with the sheep.

Lara barked three times and headlights instantly lit up the scene, dazzling the two men. A voice on a megaphone announced, 'You are surrounded, throw down the gun and give yourselves up.' There was a moment of silence broken only by a release of gas from Bill's bottom. The men did as they were told. As the police moved in a dozen sheep wandered into the light looking for their supper.

18. The Further Adventures of Spy Dog

Ben was telling his story yet again, still sounding as excited as the first time he'd recounted it. His school friends gathered around, straining to catch his every word.

'So I steadied the motorbike next to the moving lorry and she just took off, did a flying leap on to the lorry,' he told his open-mouthed friends. 'Then she ripped open the canvas and rescued my sister and cousin. And I was driving the Harley. Me and my other cousin, but me the most.'

'And what happened to the dog smugglers?' piped a voice from the back.

'Bill was caught at the scene and had no choice but to give himself up,' explained Ben. 'Then Lara jumped in the van and

brought the police all the way back to find Ned and the photographer. What an adventure!'

'And what happened to the dogs?' asked another excited voice from the audience.

'Well, we'd let them loose and loads of them actually found their way to their homes. It took the RSPCA a couple of days to round them all up, but every single one had a happy ending. The police have caught the entire gang of dognappers, so the whole operation has been closed down. Apparently Bill was only a small part of it.'

'And Ned. He was whacked about a bit. Is he OK?'

'The great news is that Ned's making a

full recovery. Lara is testifying that he helped out so, although Bill will go to prison, Ned will get another chance. And the really good news is that the bang he took has cured his stutter. Lara says she visited him in hospital yesterday and he was speaking perfectly. Says he's going to train to be a speech therapist so he can help others. He's all bandaged up but has the biggest smile on his face. Lara says he can't stop talking, as if he's making up for lost time.'

'Excellent. What about the photographer? I mean, he could publish his photos and do loads of damage. He could destroy Lara's secret.'

'Well, he woke up three days later. Professor Cortex developed his photos for him and took out the ones of Lara. Then he went to see the photographer and apparently had a quiet word. The photographer was really scared because, after all, he was planning to take some of the smugglers' money. He could have gone to jail. The professor fibbed that he would be watched by the Secret Service and, if he ever stepped out of line again, he would be sent to prison and the key thrown away.' Ben beamed brightly. 'I bet he's always looking over his shoulder, thinking he's being followed.'

Ben's audience was grinning at the thought. 'He promised never to come near Lara again. And Max has found a nice new home. He lives on a farm apparently. He's become very friendly with the sheep.'

'Fantastic, so everything ended brilliantly. Everyone was happy.'

'Not quite

everyone,' smiled Ben. 'Mum was pretty stressed by the whole thing. She saw us on the motorbike and fainted. She couldn't believe the adventure we'd got ourselves into and was furious that the professor had made Lara do a mission while we thought we were supposed to be on holiday. She's said we can never go on another holiday again. In fact, she said that since we adopted Lara we keep falling into adventures. She said we can't have any more.'

'Oh no, that's terrible. No more adventures, then?'

Ben looked across at Lara and patted her on the back. She wagged her tail hard and winked at her owner. He grinned and winked back. 'I'll work on Mum. We'll see about that.'

It all started with a Scarecrow.

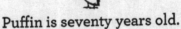

Puffin is seventy years old.

Sounds ancient, doesn't it? But Puffin has never been
so lively. We're always on the lookout for the next big
idea, which is how it began all those years ago.

Penguin Books was a big idea from the mind of
a man called Allen Lane, who in 1935 invented
the quality paperback and changed the world.
**And from great Penguins, great Puffins grew,
changing the face of children's books forever.**

The first four Puffin Picture Books were hatched in 1940 and the
first Puffin story book featured a man with broomstick arms called
Worzel Gummidge. In 1967 Kaye Webb, Puffin Editor, started the
Puffin Club, promising to **'make children into readers'**.
She kept that promise and over 200,000 children became
devoted Puffineers through their quarterly instalments of
Puffin Post, which is now back for a new generation.

Many years from now, we hope you'll look back and
remember Puffin with a smile. **No matter what your age
or what you're into, there's a Puffin for everyone.**
The possibilities are endless, but one thing is for sure:
whether it's a picture book or a paperback, a sticker book
or a hardback, **if it's got that little Puffin
on it – it's bound to be good.**